Meenakshi Kumar

---

Kaleidoscope

Vanguard Press

**VANGUARD PAPERBACK**

© Copyright 2024
**Meenakshi Kumar**

The right of Meenakshi Kumar to be identified as author of this work has been asserted by her in accordance with the Copyright, Designs and Patents Act 1988.

**All Rights Reserved**

No reproduction, copy or transmission of this publication may be made without written permission.
No paragraph of this publication may be reproduced, copied or transmitted save with the written permission of the publisher, or in accordance with the provisions of the Copyright Act 1956 (as amended).

Any person who commits any unauthorised act in relation to this publication may be liable to criminal prosecution and civil claims for damages.

A CIP catalogue record for this title is available from the British Library.

ISBN 978 1 83794 168 1

This is a work of fiction. Names, characters, businesses, places, events and incidents are either the product of the author's imagination or used in a fictitious manner. Any resemblance to actual persons, living or dead, or actual events is purely coincidental.

*Vanguard Press is an imprint of*
*Pegasus Elliot Mackenzie Publishers Ltd.*
www.pegasuspublishers.com

First Published in 2024

**Vanguard Press**
**Sheraton House  Castle Park**
**Cambridge  England**

Printed & Bound in Great Britain

This book is dedicated to the creator of this universe, the divine energy.

Heartfelt gratitude for one and all for various shades of emotional imprints that were cherished in the face of ebbs in life, and nourished when life allowed moments to revel!

In the spate of the digital and technological revolution, we are kind of losing the connection with our surroundings that nourished our souls, and have started running after materiality to gratify our senses leaving the soul and mind impoverished.

The collection of short stories aims at igniting the slumber emotions. For Gen Z, for whom there is a lot of time yet to experience feelings such as: to kindle lives or repair wounds, to fill life with the fragrance of love and happiness, and many such moments for tryst with emotions, the stories will be food for the soul. And, a new angle to look for beauty in life on this planet.

It's a moment to thank the divine for gifting us life on this beautiful planet; and to all the friends and family for giving memories galore.

# Contents

Devaki Didi ............................................................. 11

All that glitters is not gold ................................... 24

Rani Aunty .............................................................. 39

The Bosom Buddies .............................................. 45

The Rich Man ........................................................ 62

Jugaad: the innovation ........................................ 70

The Gold Chain ..................................................... 77

Beauty is only skin deep ...................................... 87

Truly yours ............................................................. 99

# Devaki Didi

Running through an uneven land, at the topmost speed, my lungs almost about to burst, feet rapidly pacing the ground, eyes searching for a safe place to hide from the view of a chasing dog. A ray of hope that lit some life back to the possibility of being saved from an impending attack, on the sight of a single house in the barren land, died almost instantly on stumbling upon a stone and being attacked by the snarling animal. As the hot blood flowed from my leg and it felt too heavy to move, my eyes opened in heebie-jeebies with a shriek. With bated breath, I looked at my feet and then around. My feet were intact.

A fat lady had crawled to make place for a few guest visitors and almost trampled my feet, also dropping some hot tea from her cup, served to her full to the brim. Though the fear of the beast was mollified, the pain from scalding due to hot tea was unbearable. There was a frenzied rush of relatives, friends, and visitors to meet the bride sitting in the adjacent room. Hardly anyone noticed the accident. After crying softly for some time, I hobbled out of that room.

I very well remembered how I revelled at the marriage; running umpteen times, adjusting my golden silk *dupatta* to hide my undeveloped chest like the grown-up girls with full breasts do, over red colour *Salwar-Kameez* (ladies dress in India and Pakistan); from the bridal room to the area beautifully decorated with roses and orchids for the reception of Baraat. As my legs began to ache, I sat on a chair and dozed off.

Someone had picked me up and placed me on the mattress of the room adjacent to the bride's, now being used as a waiting area for meeting the newly wed couple. A thick rug covered the entire length of the marble tessellate floor. Mattresses covered with white bed sheets lay along the length and breadth of the room emptied of items it housed before the function; a couch, a wooden almirah, and a few iron and aluminium boxes, all finding a temporary home in a cellar, the dark storeroom used for storage of pickles and junk. Rules of hygiene were gravely compromised. Guests falling low in the degree of consciousness walked inside with soiled footwear leaving a dusty mark with their slippers on the rug. The frown became noticeable on faces of those who had to sleep in that room, for a while, but others were less bothered because the rug did not belong to anyone. It was rented.

After a while when the pain subsided, I moved to the bridal room. The room was full of guests busy bantering with the groom and the bride. Only my glances could see over the heads of people encircling the bride to steal a look of her face, who was too engrossed to even check whether I had eaten or not.

It was my sister's wedding. She was almost 7 years older than me. For me, she was my mother, not even my second mother. Mother had two pregnancies aborted after *Devki didi* in desire of a son. After the birth of my brother,

Kundan, I descended as an unwanted child in the family, who was accidentally born with the hope to get another male child. So, I was raised by my sister. Mother had no time left for me as all her attention was on her son. All the love, emotion and energy of my parents were channelled towards raising my brother.

My belly churned and my head swirled due to hunger. I realized that I was starving, but who could have I asked to give me food? On other days *Devaki didi* used to feed me before having her food. That day, I couldn't even get a glimpse of her. On the previous night, I dozed off before the dinner started being served to *baaratis* (the guests attending marriage from the groom's side), and as per the social protocol, quite strictly adhered to in small Indian cities and districts, the guests attending the marriage function from bride's side were served dinner after the baaratis.

Adieu! It was time for *adieu*. Everyone was crying, and I cried my lungs out. The reason for the crying was different for everyone. Some cried to follow the tradition, but I cried with double the intensity because of my aching belly and fearful heart of being left alone and fending for myself. Didi was crying out with loud hiccups from behind a long veil covering her face.

The parents looked relieved. Their flow of words of praise for *Devaki didi's* husband and in-laws was like they were singing paean for a deity.

In the meanwhile, my mind was becoming a battlefield between an aching belly due to hunger and a throbbing head due to questions about my future in the house. Like the war brings only destruction, I wanted to pull down the flower strings and hit someone hard to show my anger. I was experiencing this kind of rebellion for the first time. To avoid doing anything wrong, I hurriedly walked up the stairs to go to the second storey of the house which was open space and the height provided a good view of the surrounding area.

I had overcast eyes. *Whom should I ask to feed me?* A moment later my mind shifted to *Devaki didi* and the nostalgia stuck with me. My vision was blurred and tears flowed incessantly to form into a deluge. The moment the heat of emotions settled, my eyes started burning due to rings of smoke in the air and the smell of half-burnt charcoal got into my nostrils. The smoke rose from the portable furnaces being lit to cook dinner for guests. The ascending smoke from the ground below rose against the backdrop of various shades of orange, due to the setting of the sun, bordering the blue sky.

I could perfectly estimate the evening tea time; it was the time *Devaki didi* prepared evening tea and snacks. I always remained by her side to assist her in serving the delicacies, firstly to the male family members, and what remained after fulfilling their appetite was apportioned among the female members. *Devaki didi* fed me some snacks from her share too. When I asked her for a full cup of sweetened tea, she said, 'Children should not consume tea because it can harm their tender system.' She wanted to give me milk instead, but there was not enough milk.

The milkman delivered milk that was sufficient for male members and the remaining milk was used to prepare tea that could be consumed by all. *Devaki didi* saved some milk while preparing tea and that milk she added to my teacup to make my excellent tasting milk tea with lots of sugar. I missed being pampered like a baby by my sister.

A thick shade of darkness started engulfing the colourful sky like the black blanket hiding everything from view, and the bedtime ghost stories that Grandma used to tell us started making inroads in my mind, and I rushed at top speed and made my way down the stairs.

The bride's lineage, friends and associates formed the core team of organizers. The team was busy preparing for the celebrations for many days. The organizing involved great effort. It was the involvement of the body, heart, and soul that had sapped them of all their energy by the end of the function. The overworked systems needed refurbishing. The place that seethed with vibrancy became dull with the snoring of tired bodies, lying prostrate, occupying every nook and corner of the house.

The house full of people felt comforting, now. Amidst the noise created by bantering, and giggles my thoughts were distracted for a while, but my thought was again back to my stomach making strange sounds. My mind started swirling and I realized that I had begun to lose control of my feet and was almost about to faint. I walked with languished steps to reach my mother who was busy feeding the child, the brother elder to me, insisting he should oblige her by having one more bite of the food.

I shuddered to utter a word before mother because *Devaki didi* was my cushion of protection to handle my matters, but suddenly I was exposed out of my cocoon to fight for my basic right to food.

I said, 'I'm feeling very hungry, *Maa*.'

Mother turned to look into my eyes and said in a harsh tone, 'The house is full of food. Why haven't you eaten anything? Go and eat whatever you want.'

My feeble heart was scared stiff, and almost instantaneously my eyes got welled up. My tears irritated my mother instead of softening her. She asked once again raising her voice, 'Why are you crying now? What impression do you want to give to guests, that I torture you? I don't give you food!'

By that time, I had started sobbing noisily. Mother's pitch was rising in the same proportion as the loudness of my crying.

Grandma, mom's mother, came in the room asking, 'What happened Kamini? Why is Chanda crying?'

Mother grumbled to *Nani*, 'Hundreds of people are eating in our house, but our *maharani* had nothing to eat since yesterday.'

Grandma pulled me in her lap and asked the servant to bring a food plate with every delicacy served. And then she looked towards her daughter saying, 'Kamini, don't you realise that she is a young child? How do you expect her to feed herself? All these days, Devaki was looking after her. You get all the time to feed Gopal who is older than her, but you did not even check whether someone gave Chanda food to eat or not.' But for mother it was like the water off a duck's back.

She replied, '*Amma*, she is a clever girl. She is jealous of Gopal and that is why she is creating all the fuss. Within no time she will grow up into a lady and we will have to marry her off like Devaki. If she doesn't learn to look after herself then how will she take care of a family. If she grows up untrained, then we will have to arrange for much more dowry to marry her off.'

Unlike the other ladies who nodded their heads in support of mother, Grandma had my back. She said, 'Kamini, every child comes with his or her destiny. You should be concerned about your role as a mother which should be same for your son and your daughter.' She was in a mood to give more sermons to mother, but her attention got diverted towards the servant bringing the plate filled with the delicacies.

Grandma had faced bitter experiences from her son, and it was her three daughters (Mother being one of them) who took care of her. She liked spending time with us, and her presence was like the shade of a tree for me.

Devaki didi and her husband were coming to our house after marriage for the first time. Everyone seemed quite excited. Some of the relatives who had come to attend the marriage were still around. The talk of the riches of *Devaki didi's* in-laws were doing the rounds among the guests. I waited for my dearest *Didi*, bright-eyed and bushy-tailed.

And there she was being the cynosure of everyone in the house. She looked completely changed, not just externally but something within her had also changed. Her hair was nicely pinned up forming a bun at the back of her head, wisps of hair formed into ringlets, and the centre parting was filled with a broad line of red vermillion. She was all decked out in diamonds and gold jewellery. A big red round *bindi* was put between her eyebrows and a dash of kohl lined up the lower edge of her eyes. Her face glowed and a hue of light pink marked the cheeks of her fair, slender face. She was surrounded by the ladies, some of whom had come from the neighbours' house just to meet her. She was busy answering the ladies whose questions were just to estimate the riches of her in-laws. *Didi's* eyes sparkled talking about the affluence of her new house and our mother drew an extra sense of pride finding the ladies jealous of her daughter's prosperity.

I kept looking at her from the corner of the wall next to the door waiting for her to ask for me even once so that I could go and hug her and narrate to her what happened after she left. But she was too engrossed in her new world. Didi's expression of rapture was the cause of pride for members in our family and also the cause of envy for neighbours. My parents were deciding to start looking for a match for me of the same stature as my sister, and I often saw them discussing that very soon they would be on their mission for groom hunting as the younger the bride, the better were the chances of a good deal.

It was to my good fortune that I was not growing as pretty as my sister. And God sent the much needed support at this juncture in the form of a senior secondary girls' school in our area. There was no girls' school earlier so most girls were uneducated like *Devaki didi*. Only a few fortunate girls born to broad-minded and affluent parents were sent for education at boarding schools in nearby cities.

It was my *Nani* (Grandma) who insisted I was enrolled in the school which also brought incentives to my parents by way of cash transfers in my name for bearing the expense of my books, uniform, and conveyance. Mother managed to save money from the government allowance given to me, and spent it on my brother.

But, for me, the school breathed new life. I enjoyed studying. At school, it felt like there was an opening for fresh air and light to seep into my life. I found new friends, who gave a lift to my spirit when I first joined the school. The girls of my age with soft voices and chubby hands were my treasures in life, and I thought that spending time with them was my greatest pleasure. We even had small fights, but altogether my life became full of happiness, and I longed for nothing more than to do well in my studies.

I performed better than my brother in all classes and started getting regular scholarships. Though *Gopal bhai* was three years older than me, we were in the same class by the time we reached high school.

*Devaki didi* was pregnant and came to stay with us. This was her third pregnancy. Her first two pregnancies were aborted miscarried because her tender system did not support the load of the baby, and to top it all she had to work her fingers to the bone doing household chores even during her pregnancy days. *Devaki didi* did not look her age any more. She looked frail and her beautiful face began to show fine lines. At the age of twenty-four, she looked like a fifty-year-old lady. She no longer looked like my sweet and beautiful *Didi*.

*Didi's* in-laws and her husband were ruthless with her. Her weak system could not bear a load of work and pregnancy together. One day she fell unconscious, and the doctor advised complete bed rest. So, she was sent to her parents' house because her husband and his family were not ready to take responsibility for *Didi*.

I had my board exams, and despite that, I made sure I was by her side for all her needs. *Devaki didi* shared that after only few days of marriage most servants were removed and it was Didi doing most of the household work. On top of that, she had to hear the taunts of her husband and in-laws that she belonged to a family with low financial status. They always gave the impression that *Devaki didi* should consider herself fortunate that she was married to their family. *Devaki didi* said, 'I used to think that I would have considered myself fortunate had the family thought me to be a human being.' She used to console herself as she was repaying some bad deeds of her past life.

My exams were over and I came back happily thinking that I would be able to spend time with *didi* without any pressure of studies lingering in my mind.

I entered the home to quite a number of guests sipping tea with my parents. *Devaki didi* was not there. Father introduced me to the guests with great aplomb as their bright, promising, and highly skilled daughter. The speck of pride raising its head like a monster immediately subsided thinking about *Devaki didi*. Hadn't *Devaki didi* done as well or maybe better than me had she been given an opportunity?

I was sitting with *Devaki didi* on the roof under the starlit sky. Mother called loudly and asked us to be with everyone sitting in the lounge. When we reached the lounge, the parents were talking in a whispering tone amongst themselves. They made us sit comfortably near them. Mother announced that after two days the groom's family, to whom I was introduced after getting home from school, were to visit our house with their boy for finalizing the marriage deal.

The information came as a bolt from the blue and it caught me on the back foot. I almost shouted, 'What! I cannot marry now. I want to study further.'

Mother came near me and said, 'Chanda, the people are very affluent, much more than Devaki's in-laws. We are fortunate to get such a good proposal for our daughters.'

But I had decided that whatever may come my way, I would not get married without completing my education.

I dreaded leading my life like Didi. I thought that it was better to end my life than to die every day. Now, it was my father's turn to give me arguments in favour of the proposal. But all arguments fell on deaf ears so far as changing my heart for getting married was concerned.

*Devaki didi* watched quietly, but as soon as the realisation dawned to her that I was losing ground before my parents, she chimed in. 'No! Chanda should not be married against her wishes. With her education and the bright future ahead of her, she is richer than the prospective groom because she owns the greatest wealth of education. Please,' she addressed our parents with folded hands, 'do not impoverish her by snatching away her dreams. Why do you consider girls as burden?'

Looking at Mother she said, 'Maa, you are also a woman. Don't you have a lesson in the form of my ruined life? Instead of supporting your daughters, you try to get rid of all connections with them. What is it that makes you resentful towards girls? Don't you bear the same pain while delivering, irrespective of the sex of the child? Please be our strength and don't be our enemy by standing against us, because society tells you so.'

My parents kept looking at *Devaki didi's* face. She had never raised her voice before. She was so gentle that people used to eat out of her hand. Our parents were dumbfounded and they gave in before our insistence.

We lost *Devaki didi*. She died due to complications during the birth of the child leaving behind a beautiful daughter. Her husband refused to take custody of his daughter, and in this way, he did me a favour as it made me feel that *Devaki didi* was with me in the guise of a child whom we called Simi.

My zeal towards studies increased manifold. I came out with flying colours in my Civil Service examination, I opted for a hometown posting, and brought my parents to stay with me along with my niece Simi. Gopal bhaiya was never good at studies, so my parents got him settled by helping him start a shop with all their savings.

I got Simi admitted to the best school in the city. I decided to provide Simi with every facility which *Devaki didi* could not get because of being a girl.

# All that glitters is not gold

Malini sat on the fourth-row aisle seat on the right side of the chartered bus. The seat, meant for three persons, had to be shared by four, as the bus was always full beyond its normal capacity, quite a common sight in the overpopulated nation.

Malini, uneasy, tried to look relaxed, after the fourth lady perched in. With closed eyes, she focussed on the lyrics of the song playing on the bus. But the bus halted again. *The bus has already picked up the passengers from its last stop so why has it stopped now?* Malini thought. She softly opened her eyes and saw some people climbing up the bus steps. Passengers started fretting, showing their unwillingness; the limited space had to be shared with unfamiliar faces. The organizer appeased them, with folded hands, to adjust for a few days.

Malini's heart skipped a beat the moment she gazed at the last person to walk in. Malini asked herself, *Oh! Tushar, how come he is in this chartered bus?* Tushar's family had recently moved to her neighbourhood. She first met him when he came with the invite to their housewarming party. At the get-together, their parents met like long-lost friends, though for Malini and Tushar, it was a first conscious meeting. It was during the function she came to know that her parents and Tushar's parents, Mrs and Mr Mitra, were close friends, and they lived near each other before Tushar's parents were relocated from Delhi. At that time, she was just a baby a few months old and Tushar a toddler; both were too young to register memories. And after years, Tushar's parents came back to Delhi and, by chance, they had their residence in the same area where Malini's parents had purchased their house.

By this time Tushar had walked in to stand near the first row of seats, and looked inside the bus, maybe in search of a vacant seat. And his roving eyes got stuck on Malini, who forced a smile to concede that he was known to her. She learnt for the first time that smiling too required an effort; all through the years of her existence on this Earth, she had greeted everyone with her spontaneous grin. But this time the feeling was strange. Her heart was beating vigorously.

The scenes of the housewarming party started playing before her eyes. The *extra attention* that Tushar paid to her had made her feel quite uncomfortable. Though he was just telling her about his latest job, his office, and the problem he faced in commuting because of his office being situated at a far off location from their area etcetera, still she was getting conscious of the envious glances of other young girls present there. Malini could not sleep after coming back from the party. Tushar's face kept on hovering before her eyes. Though she was quite used to the special favours of beaus, she had never been so restless ever before. With much difficulty, she got some sleep in the early morning hours. Thankfully, it was the weekend the next day.

All the effort to get a grip on her weakening emotions was foiled the moment her eyes again met Tushar's in the chartered bus. *Oh, I am falling prey to this stupid emotion; maybe this is what people call love. It's a weakening emotion. No, I can't let it happen to me!* She breathed deeply to take resolve and tried regaining her composure. She didn't want to wear her heart on her sleeve.

*I don't want to look like a fool. He is our old family friend, and I need to show some courtesy at least.* Malini reprimanded herself. *But how can I make him feel comfortable?* she thought. The jam-packed bus did not allow movement even one step further. She lifted her eyelids to look at Tushar once again, Maybe, she wanted to acknowledge her helplessness. But her glance led her into further turmoil; Tushar was making payment to the person collecting the bus fare. After making the payment, he looked towards her and gestured that he was paying for her too. She mildly shook her head to refuse his favour, but he smiled gently suggesting that she should be cool. His destination was before hers. He got off the bus leaving a trail of tumultuous emotions for Malini.

Malini heaved a sigh, a long one. She felt annoyed at herself for not being able to avoid him paying for her. Though the amount was not much, it meant being weighed down with obligation. All through the day she kept thinking of ways to return his money and decided to do it on the weekend. *Yeah, the weekend should be the ideal time*, she thought.

The next day too, it happened the same way. Tushar's stop came last during the bus's morning route, so he could get a little place to stand near the front seat row. And the collection always began from the front. So whenever he was making the payment, he paid for her as well. But surprisingly, she did not feel as much indignation the next day and by the third day, she accepted it gladly, as she had decided that she would be settling her dues by going with her mother to his house, on the weekend.

The first thing she did on the weekend was to rush to her mother to narrate the entire week's story. She was getting restless to unload her burden, but the moment she had to talk about Tushar, she fumbled. *Well, I will make some excuse in the evening and take Mom to Tushar's house*, she decided.

She enjoyed her favourite afternoon siesta during weekends, which she would not miss in any circumstance. She was still in bed, and the doorbell chimed to disturb her sleep. With a lot of reluctance, rubbing her eyes, she walked towards the door to open it. And when she saw Tushar at the door, she rubbed her eyes again to ensure that she was not dreaming.

She hurriedly opened the door. Her mussed up hair covered some part of her face, her half-open eyes were still red, and her mind was dazed; she didn't know what to do next. She forced her eyes to open and looked towards him; his eyes were fixed on her. Malini's cheeks became pink, and she shifted her glance to welcome him into the house saying, 'Oh, hi! I hope you didn't have to wait long?'

Tushar walked in smiling. Instead of answering her question, he asked, 'Hello Malini! I hope I am not disturbing you, people, by coming at the wrong time?'

Instead of Malini, her mother answered, as she had walked behind Malini to check at the door. 'Tushar, you are almost like a family to us. How can we be disturbed by you? It is our pleasure that you have come to visit us.' Mother must have spoken those words as a courtesy for a family friend, but it reddened Malini's face, and she rushed towards the kitchen to hide her discomfiture under the pretext to get water for Tushar.

Malini offered the glass of water to Tushar. Mrs Sen, Malini's mother, said, 'Malini, come, sit and chat with Tushar, I shall get some snacks and tea.' She patted at the chair adjacent to Tushar's. Malini smilingly obeyed her mother.

Only two of them were there, and both remained quiet looking into each other's eyes. Malini relished every moment of that quietude. She wished those moments could be prolonged, or freeze so that she could store them and relive them whenever she felt like doing it, but her mother came in with a well-laid tray full of eatables. Malini forgot to talk about the bus fare, even then.

After a week, Tushar stopped coming to her chartered bus. But her eyes searched for him whenever people walked in from his stop. Tushar's presence made her boring journey enjoyable.

One day Malini missed her bus because of an urgent meeting that lasted a bit late in the evening. So, the only option she had was to board a DTC bus. The bus was only halfway through when it had to discontinue its journey due to some technical glitch in the engine. Malini, frustrated and flummoxed, got down along with other passengers to look for another bus. She dreaded hiring an auto-rickshaw all alone at dusk because of the high incidences of rape and robbery cases in the capital city. While she waited at the stop, it began to drizzle which made people huddle closer, trying to get inside the shelter of the bus stand. Malini clasped her handbag and the office folder tightly between both arms which rested on her breasts. She had bent her head to let raindrops fall on her instead of the file.

The constant honking distracted her attention. She looked up, and it was Tushar pressing the car horn. Seeing him at the stop made her get some confidence back. She rushed and almost barged into the car and sat beside Tushar. Tushar pressed the car's accelerator and smiled looking at her, as she was still recovering from the feeling of getting lost in the crowd. After the car started moving, she realized that she had got in without Tushar's permission. Maybe he just wanted to check with her as to what she was doing there, she thought. But Tushar had no expression on his face.

Malini wanted Tushar to say something, or even ask her anything, but he remained tight-lipped. The best he did was to turn his head towards her with a smile. He dropped her a little away from their residence to avoid being seen together which could ignite and fuel rumours.

After reaching home she opened the refrigerator to take out the water bottle, and there she found her favourite sweets in the fridge. Mom told her that Mrs Mitra had sent the sweets because Tushar had bought a new car.

*Oh... so it was his new car. It must be Tushar suggesting that the sweets be sent to my house.* She casually once mentioned to him that she loved only this sweet and nothing else. But why couldn't he tell her about that? *And look at me; how stupid I am. I didn't say thanks to him for dropping me home. I don't understand what goes wrong with me whenever he is around. But what is wrong with him; he is so confident otherwise. Maybe he has too much of an attitude*, she thought. But she really treasured his reticence and cool mannerisms.

She had to stay late in the office, as she had to finish an important presentation. Travelling at late hours appeared like braving a horror movie. Her legs were trembling while walking towards the bus stop. It could sound strange to people that a modern, independent, and highly qualified girl could be so timid in her heart. But this is how she was. She kept pace with the world but also was conscious of the fact that it was still a man's world. She was murmuring to herself, 'Getting a chartered bus is a remote possibility, even getting a DTC bus for my route seems impossible. Does that mean I have to hire an auto? OMG! I should have asked the boss to drop me home. But would it have been proper?'

With negative thoughts clouding her mind, she walked ponderously towards the stop. After a while, she felt that she was being followed by a car; the car stopped quite close to her. An unknown fear gripped her badly. The thought of getting kidnapped by the goons made her react instantaneously. She gathered herself for running hard to the police booth near the stop. She had just begun to run when a familiar voice calling her name made her halt and turn her head to look towards the voice source. Tushar's car followed her at a slow speed. He rolled down the car window to call her name aloud. 'Why are you running away? Come in!' And he unlocked the car door to let her in. Her heart was beating like a fast running train engine. He offered her the water bottle and asked her to chill out.

But he still didn't ask her anything. After a few minutes, when she looked comfortable, he asked Malini to select an audio cassette from the car locker and insert it in the stereo. Malini took out the cassette after reading the track names and was about to insert it when Tushar cupped her hand and helped her slide the cassette into the stereo as if she was a child. The touch of Tushar's hand had the effect of a mild electric shock; a sweet tingling sensation ran through her body that made her immobile for some seconds. She was not sure whether Tushar did it deliberately, or he thought that Malini didn't know how to use a car stereo.

A piece of soft music started playing making the mood quite romantic. Malini wanted Tushar to do some talking, to speak up, about anything. But he remained engrossed in music and driving. Malini was becoming impatient. *Why does he not speak to me? Why does he not ask me anything? How to read his mind? Does he consider me just a friend?* It was becoming too suffocating. Even the soft music appeared as noise because of questions in her mind struggling to know the answer.

And, finally, when it became difficult to bear his silence, she blurted out, 'How can you be so cool and unperturbed?'

He looked towards her with a sparkle in his eyes, as if he expected her to make this complaint, and said, 'You have also been so all through, Malini, calm, unaffected.'

Malini had nothing to say. In her heart, she was saying, 'Can you not read my eyes? Don't you hear my heart talking to you?' She read in all romantic stories that love birds don't need a language to communicate. God gives them an added power to comprehend unspoken words, the language of eyes and heart. Maybe these facts remain true only for the characters in the story, which is a creation of the writers, and for God's creations God has equipped them with various abilities hence they are expected to use these faculties to the best of their advantage.

Tushar, after a while, said, 'Malini,' and Malini's low spirit had some energy back. She turned her head to look at him. His hands resting confidently on the car's steering and eyes set on the road ahead, he spoke with authority in his voice. 'You will have to compromise with your career,' he said and applied the car brakes. They were close to her house.

Malini was befuddled. She got out saying, 'Thanks,' this time. Malini kept walking steadily towards her house with Tushar's words still ringing in her ears. She was trying to decipher his feelings from his words.

As she stepped into the house, she overheard her parents discussing some marriage proposals. And, while having dinner, Mrs Sen proudly repeated whatever Malini heard her talking about when she was back from the office. It was obvious that she wanted Malini to know about the proposals.

Mrs Sen was telling her husband, 'All the proposals are worth consideration.'

'It had to be! After all, it is difficult to find a girl like our daughter,' Mr Sen said.

'Ma, I must study further. I don't want to get married now.' Malini sulked after her father left the table.

'But we are just evaluating good proposals. We are not marrying you off immediately. And we will not do anything without your consent, that much I assure you. If you don't like anything about the guy or his family, there will be no pressure from our side,' Mrs Sen said.

Malini's face still looked sad.

'Do you like Tushar?' Mother asked.

And his name made her burst into giggles. 'But I never said that!' Malini rushed to her room saying this. And Mrs Sen understood her daughter's choice. She smiled. After discussing with her husband, she invited Tushar and his family for dinner at their house.

Malini prepared the sweet dish for dinner. Everyone liked the food, especially the sweet dish. Mrs Mitra praised Malini a lot. Mrs Sen thought that it an appropriate moment to share her mind and said, 'Our families can bond stronger if we think of changing our friendship into a relationship.' And she looked towards Tushar and Malini to suggest what she intended. Tushar smiled, but Mrs Mitra did not take the idea well. She immediately made an excuse and left with her family. While leaving, Tushar stood in front of Malini and looked into her eyes for a few seconds, as if to assure her that everything would be all right.

For two days there was no communication from Tushar's family. Though subtle, the message was clear. Still, Mrs Sen called up Mrs Mitra to know their answer in clear cogent words. Malini was sitting near her mother flipping through a magazine. She sat close enough to overhear the voice of the person on another end of the telephone. Mrs Mitra was telling her mother that they were considering a proposal of a girl for Tushar. She eschewed talking about the issue that Mrs Sen had raised during dinner.

Mrs Sen could read Malini's mind and as her daughter's spokesperson asked, 'Is Tushar ready for the proposal?'

Mrs Mitra said, 'Of course, he is ready to meet the girl. And a final yes or no can be possible only after the meeting.'

'Okay!' Mrs Sen almost banged the phone down.

Malini pretended to be nonchalant, but she was shaken violently inside. Whenever she was alone, tears flowed as if they could heal her wounded heart. The broken heart pierced her soul bringing alive the memory spells; moments spent with Tushar caused a shadow, and made her plunge into everlasting gloom. She felt shattered. At every stop she carefully watched the passengers walking in, wishing that Tushar might board the bus to share about the family pressure he was facing. She would have appreciated him for his honesty all through her life. Her faith in human values was shaken. Her idolized concept of love didn't let her face reality.

Basically, you cannot trade something which does not exist. There is no place for genuine emotions in our world because it cannot be quantified in material terms. So, it was all her fault. She expected something which did not exist. Tushar was just flirting with her like he must have been doing with other girls. Or maybe Tushar was too cowardly to face his mother and take a definite stand in her favour, and again this meant that he lacked the feeling of true love that Malini had for him. She wanted to unload, but she could not share her story with anybody. She didn't want her story to fall on undeserving ears and spread around like wildfire causing harm to her parents' reputation. She already felt the culprit for bringing insult to her family because of her tacit but immature demand.

'Malini.' Her mother was talking. 'You are a crazy girl. We have such nice proposals waiting for you. Tushar and his family stand nowhere in comparison to these proposals, but you have gone blind for him. It was just because we saw both of you interested in each other that I touched on the topic. Maybe Tushar could not oppose his family. But a guy who cannot assert for you now will never be able to stand for you. Honestly speaking, we never were in favour of considering Tushar for this proposal. Our daughter is a princess and she deserves a young man who is a prince in the true sense.'

Malini kept listening to her mother quietly. She felt too exhausted emotionally for any logic to work for her. And she left it to her parents to choose her life partner.

After evaluating all proposals her parents selected Raghav. And the way events unfolded, everything appeared to be pre-decided, proving our ancient theory that "matches are made in heaven" correct. Malini was a bit apprehensive in the beginning, but later she found that her in-laws were much better than her expectation. The affectionate nature of Raghav and his parents belied the "terror house" image of the in-laws' place.

Raghav had an excellent combination of a loving heart and a brilliant mind. His boldness and daring made her feel protected, and the way he cared for the smallest of her needs made her feel like a princess of her beautiful world.

After her honeymoon, Malini went to spend a few days with her parents. She, while chatting with her mother, came to know that Tushar's family had moved from their neighbourhood to a new apartment. Tushar got married to the girl of Mrs Mitra's choice. The dowry that Tushar's wife fetched and their unmatching pair was the talk of the town. Mrs Sen became busy with her household chores and Malini sat ruminating about her past days.

She asked herself, wasn't she nurturing two contrasting desires: Tushar, and her pledge that she would not marry the person who demanded dowry. *And maybe dowry was the first criterion of negotiation for Tushar's marriage. Even if Tushar was not in favour of the dowry, he was very much a part of his family, and to exist by breaking links with family is a very difficult decision. And then, who knows that Tushar was very much a part of his family's decision, as apples don't fall far from the tree!*

Malini thanked her parents; her eyes looked up to look at the sky to thank the invisible force, the god, for leading her life towards the right direction. How she had felt at one point in time that she could not live without Tushar, but after meeting Raghav and his family she felt that she could not have wished for a better life.

It is a tragedy with we humans that we assess the worth of a person to the extent allowed by our sensory perceptions which have their limitations in measuring only the external material aspects. The attributes of love, compassion and the sensitivity to perceive emotions behind simple gestures are indeed the gauges to assess the intrinsic worth and value of a person. It was not the bus fare that bothered Malini so much as the feeling that someone cared for her beyond material consideration. She misunderstood the courtesy being offered by the neighbour as the genuine emotion of love.

Her mind was being assailed by the old memories and she decided to bring peace to herself as fast as she could.

She woke up a bit early the next morning and joined her parents for morning tea. She felt completely at peace, and with small steps, she walked out of the house for a ramble to a nearby park. She meandered on the lanes within the colony to reach the park. It was almost office time and the chartered buses crisscrossed picking up passengers for different office routes. Suddenly, a white chartered bus crossed from her side. This was the same bus on which she used to commute to her office. She stood watching the chartered bus move away from her sight and heaved a sigh of relief.

Malini went back home and then she went to Tushar's house with her mother with a precious, beautiful gift for Tushar and his wife to unload the heavy burden of "unpaid fares". But Tushar had left his parents to stay with his in-laws' to manage his father-in-law's business. Malini left the gift with Tushar's mom and returned home much lighter after unloading her burden on her heart.

Malini thanked her lucky stars for saving her from being part of a mean family.

# Rani Aunty

I was hurriedly taking bites from mouth-melting, freshly prepared muffins when Mom called out to check whether I had taken my bath or not.

'Mum... I'm o...oing...' I said with some effort, making an attempt to prevent the food falling out of my mouth, and finding it difficult to speak as my mouth was full to almost its maximum capacity.

Saying this, I rushed towards the bathroom as I was fully aware that Mom would not wait an extra second to go to the opening of Rani auntie's new muffin store, and I could have missed being part of the fun party at the new store.

This store was a part of the dream project of Rani aunty who wished to create a space in the city where families could spend some moments in peace. There was a play area with few nannies to take care of kids, while the couples could get a dose of freshness and enjoy delectable shakes, healthy salads, and yummy cakes, with of course its signature dish, the muffins, the store speciality.

Mom had taken leave from her bank for the opening, and her leave was fully justified because she was the one who had to cut the ribbon and declare the store open. This would raise anxiety in the mind of readers to know more about Mom, because one needs to be a public figure having risen to the status of a celebrity to announce the beginning of an important event in someone's life.

Mom occupied a place higher than any celebrity in Rani auntie's life. Then, it was also not a long-nurtured relationship; it all started just six years back.

We had gone to spend our holidays at our granny's house. Usually, Grandpa and Grandma would come to Delhi during our holidays because it was difficult for Mom and Dad to manage leave. Then it was a good change for our grandparents to come out of their traditional home and stay with us.

When Granny became seriously ill then there was no option left for my parents than to be at Granny's side and look after her. Dad stayed for a week and once Granny started recovering, he left because he had a project getting delayed due to his absence. Mom decided to stay back with me and my sister to take care of Granny.

Granny had a good support system of servants and a whole big family of neighbours, who were always ready to help with her problems and celebrate the joys of life.

Granny's illness had made our house a hub for get togethers in the evenings. The male members, after being back from work and accompanied by their wives, would come to our house to enquire about Granny's health.

At a place where electricity shows up just like an item number in a movie, gossiping serves as the most important source of entertainment. So, Granny's illness became an opportunity to grab a few moments of entertainment for all the well-wishers of our dear granny. This opportunity provided benefits like the package deal on a product; people coming to enquire about Granny's health would have tea, snacks and gossip free in a cool room where an inverter operated fan and light would work when all other houses would be lit by the light of lanterns.

Rajani's marriage occupied the top of the gossip column of all visitors. There was a clear division of groups on this topic. Those in favour of Rajani were from pro-woman groups and called themselves modernists; their faces gleamed when they praised Rajani for her guts. They said, 'Rajani has proved that nowadays girls are no less than boys.'

Another group was staunchly against the freedom of women and quoted scriptures to prove that women were lesser mortals and intellectually low in comparison to men. They said, 'Rajani should not have rejected the proposal. Now, who will marry this girl? Moreover, she could have had the support of her husband to look after the family.'

The pro-Rajani group said, 'What if the son-in-law refused to look after her family? Poor Rajani would have been in no position to do anything for her bereaved family.'

Somebody would say, 'You see if she crosses her marriageable age there would be...'

And the discussion would go on and on until Granny would intervene. This was becoming a *sine qua non* of every day's *tête à tête*.

Mom was curious to know more about Rajani, but if she expressed her anxiety in public then she risked marring her professional status, which even Granny wouldn't appreciate. Mom's professional qualifications and her status of working as a manager in a public sector bank had added a star in the status of my grandparents because in a small and remote district of Uttar Pradesh, there were hardly any women qualified beyond a graduation degree, especially in Granny's known circle of well-wishers.

Finally, one day when all guests had left, Mom, hardly able to control her curiosity, asked Grandma about Rajani.

Rajani was the daughter of *Postmaster saab*, the village postman, who died of a heart attack a few months back. Rajani was a beautiful and intelligent girl who was top in her university in her subject. After the death of her father, Rajani refused to get married to the boy with whom she was already engaged.

The reason for not marrying was that she knew well that her father's savings were the only resource left for the family to survive, and her marriage would cost her family the entire savings and even much more. How could have she left her family in the lurch after her father's death? She decided to support her two younger brothers and mother rather than leave them and be at the mercy of her husband and his family.

She had started taking tuition and looked for a decent job to support her family. Unlike metro cities, employment opportunities and especially for a woman are almost negligible in smaller places.

By listening to people's discussion we had already developed a soft spot for Rajani, and her story moved Mom deep inside her heart. The next day, Mom took directions for Rajani's house from a servant, and after dinner, we decided to take a stroll so that we could meet Rajani.

In the thatched roofed, dimly lit house there were a few children sitting on chairs facing a pretty girl sitting across the table. She had big, beautiful eyes, and a fair complexion. Her long hair formed into a loose lock near her nape. The serenity on her face glowing in the light of a lantern was no less than the glow on the face of a beauty queen.

Mom did not like to disturb her that day. The next day she called for her and offered to get her a job in Delhi. Rajani's family had no objection because my mother's credentials were well known to everyone in the *muhallah* (colony).

Rajani became our favourite Rani aunty and came with us to Delhi. Mom got her a job as an assistant in a private company. With Mom's efforts, she could get a place in the women's hostel. Rani aunty was interested in cooking so she attended a baking course during her weekends.

Thereafter, she started a mini outlet of snacks that she would operate on the weekends. It instantly became a hit and began the story of Rani's bakery.

One after another, franchisee stores were opened. Now the dream store of Rani Aunty was to start. In six years, her life had changed completely. Both her brothers were settled; one went abroad and another qualified for an officer's post in the government

Then *Mr. Perfect* arrived in her life, a well settled handsome boy who fell completely for Rani auntie's looks, and of course the taste of her muffins. With Mom's permission she got engaged to him and her marriage was due after the opening of her dream store. Her mother stayed with her and she would continue to do so even after she got married.

For Rani aunty, Mom occupied the place of an angel who did magic to her life.

*Sometimes we need just the support of a helping hand and the rest of the journey happens...*

# The Bosom Buddies

Shyamli, after a long summer vacation, waited impatiently to be with her friends at school.

Lying on the bed adjacent to a window in her room, she gazed at stars littered in the sky which looked like a million candles lit on a *Diwali day*. Turning sideways, with both hands tucked beneath her head on the pillow, she slipped into her land of dreams in no time.

The grilled iron gates of the school strictly followed the hands of the clock and remained open till 7:30 a.m. Within the school precincts, there existed an environment which was in complete contrast to the outside mundane world. The world within the school boundaries comprised young girls with eyes full of beautiful dreams. They were least aware of the wider corrupt world of which they would have to become part after their school days are over. The societal norms would be much harder for them because they belonged to the female gender of the human species.

Shyamli reached school a little before time. As per her expectation, she found Paramjeet waiting for her eagerly and it was her wait that made her feel special at the school. Paramjeet's presence in school made the school appear a beautiful place to her.

The moment Param's roving eyes caught glimpse of Shyamli stepping in through the giant school entrance gate, she ran towards her by pulling herself away from the Doric columns on which she leaned casually near the convent. Paramjeet grabbed Shyamli in a cuddle like long lost friends meeting after ages.

Paramjeet and Shyamli both had endless stocks of gossip accumulated during the vacation, and they both began blabbing as fast as they could. Then they realized that their words collided like two trains running on the same track from opposite directions. Now both wanted the other to speak their story and finish, but by the time they could decide who would speak first, they had reached their class. Shyamli deposited her bag next to Paramjeet's.

Being in the class meant observing the decorum of the class, hence no talking. Shamli and Paramjit were punished many times for their talkativeness and had been warned against it. 'If you both are found talking again you would be made to sit at different desks,' the teacher had warned them. Paramjeet and Shamli had been friends from the first day in school when they came with their parents for the admission interview.

Shamli, looked sideways, to check the corridor, which led to the staff room from where teachers moved out to take charge of their respective classes. With no teacher in sight, she felt quite safe, and stealthily slipped her hand into Paramjeet's bag to take charge of her tiffin box. She pulled open the tiffin box's cover to sneak a peek at its contents. And the excitement took the better of her; the wide grin, dilated eyes and puckered lips were good enough gestures to suggest that the food in the tiffin matched Shamli's expectation! Before Param could speak a word, Shamli had put the tiffin box back, and moved her face closer to Paramjeet's to plant a kiss on her cheek.

'What are you doing?' Paramjeet asked. She looked to check if anyone noticed them doing that.

'Param,' Shamli asked, 'did you get my message that I sent you via stars to get my favourite food in your tiffin today, the stuffed *Aloo*-paratha (Indian bread stuffed with mashed potatoes) with pickles? No one cooks it the way your mom does.'

Before any reply from Param, the teacher came into the classroom. They rose with the rest of the class to greet the teacher who entered from the door opposite to the expected one, after finishing her lecture in the adjacent class.

The look of her loved food stoked Shamli's hunger. All her attention was focused on the sound coming from near the belfry arch where the bell was mounted; only after the striking of the bell would tiffin time start. Then she also wanted to have her favourite food at the most desired location, under the shade of the banyan tree.

Shamli took over Paramjeet's tiffin before running for their preferred place and handed over hers to Paramjeet saying, 'Param, please allow me to be selfish. I cannot let you share from your own tiffin. I'm sure you can have this food after going back to your house.'

After comfortably squatting below the shade of the banyan tree, Paramjeet smiled and said, 'Not a bad idea Shamli. Even I am bored with my mom's cooking.' And it was Param's turn to open the tiffin to check what Shamli brought.

Even before Paramjeet could open Shamli's box, the reverberation of the school's public address system caught their attention and it was followed the school principal's voice.

'All the girls kindly get back to their classes. No one should move out of their class until further order.'

'What happened?' The girls looked at each other's faces to find out the answer, but no one had any clues.

'Maybe the class teacher will know.' With similar thoughts, the girls moved towards their respective classes susurrating amongst themselves. The rustling due to the movement of girls settled, but the air was still full of unheard noise; probably this was the heaviness of negative and scary thought waves within the minds of the girls. There was an intermittent sound of thumps and thuds; Paramjeet instantly recognized the sound and whispered in Shamli's ear, 'It is the sound of bullets firing.'

The rest of the class was still unsure as to what was going on. The girls, with blank expression, looked at each other, and the suspense lasted till the teacher announced in a tone as low as she could, after bolting all the doors to stop the entry of any outsider, 'Girls, don't be scared. We will all fight it together.'

'What happened, ma'am?' one of the girls asked putting all the strength in her voice.

'Terrorists have attacked our area. The sound that you can hear is the sound of the exchange of bullets between the police and those terrorists. And we know just that from the gatekeeper. It is quite possible that they might enter our premises. So, at this difficult moment, we all need to pray and maintain our calm. Don't be scared, preserve your strength and we will fight them together if we are attacked.'

The faces of girls were white with fear. Paramjeet, putting a brave face on, said, 'Don't worry, girls, my father and his daring men are going to put up a tough fight. I can assure you that the attackers will bite the dust before they dare to enter our school premises. And don't even be afraid of these sounds, I mean sound of the bullets firing. I have heard it so many times during my father's training camps.' Param's words of courage made a momentary impact like the sun briefly exposing itself to view during a chilly, snowy winter day.

The doors on both sides of the room provided cooling due to wind circulation. Since all the doors in the classroom were bolted, and there were no windows in the class, it was only the fan connected to the ceiling that offered some respite by rotating constantly. The girls, with the teacher's permission, had huddled together to allay the cloud of fear generating within their minds. They clamped each other's hands in tight grips and shivered due to fear on a hot Indian summer day.

Time progressed with great difficulty. It was only after the scary sound of bullet exchange subsided, the clasp of girls' hands loosed, and their breathing was back to normal. The speaker hanging above the blackboard also confirmed the situation was back to normal. The news had spread like the forest fire and parents and guardians of students had started pouring in with concern and apprehension to pick their wards. And the students whose parents had not come were allowed to make phone calls to their homes.

Param's house was near the police post, hardly a kilometre away from school. Her father was a senior police officer, and he was allotted government accommodation near the post he oversaw. Usually, she used to walk down to her home, or her mom came to pick her up.

Shamli's house was quite far off. Her house was on the city's outskirts. Since there was a strict instruction that no one could go back home alone, Param too thought of calling up her mom, but Shamli stopped her from doing so.

'It's okay, Param. My parents are coming to pick me up, and we can drop you off on our way. In the meanwhile, we can have a little more time to be together,' Shamli said reflecting excitement in her voice.

Param and Shamli sat in a corner waiting for Shamli's parents to arrive. The situation appeared back to normal and both the girls became oblivious to the scare, of that dreadful moment, when death seemed to have approached so close that it sent a chill down their spine.

'Param, I can see that sweet smile and I want to know the reason behind it,' Shamli said.

'How do you know that I have a secret to share?' Param asked.

'If you have a broken eyelash falling on your cheek, who sees that first, and picks it up to give it to you to blow that away and ask for a wish, me or you?' Shamli said.

'Of course, it is you!' Param said.

Shamli chuckled. 'Then? Can I not read your eyes and know your emotions?' Shamli asked.

'Yes, Shamli, you are right! Since morning I wanted to share this secret with you. Anyway, let me share it now before your parents arrive and pick us up. Shamli,' Param said looking at Shamli, 'I am in a dilemma, baby. I never got so confused about my own thoughts. It is a bit strange that I am not able to identify my own feelings.'

'Param, will you please share the actual story or do you intend to while away all the time we have together?' Shamli said with a bit of irritation. 'Only if you share the facts I can help you, darling.' Shyamli added to hide her agitation as she wanted to know the story before her parents arrived.

'Yeah! Correct!' Param replied with a smile understanding the love behind her friend's ire. 'Now listen to my story. His name is Kanav. His family moved to our neighbourhood only a month back, and I came to know about them only when Kanav came from the hostel to spend his vacation. He is a final-year student of medicine.

'And it happened like this. I casually stood on my terrace watching vehicles on the road when a car stopped in front of our neighbours' house. A young, dashing person got out of the car to open the gate to let his car in, and his first look took my breath away. The very next day we bumped into each other in the park and instantly became friends. Being next-door neighbours, it hardly took any time for our families to become friends and Kanav became a favourite of my parents too. He plans to go to the USA for his higher studies so he might stay there during his vacations for his preparations for the tests to apply for masters at US universities.

'Dad requested him to help me in my mathematics while he was here. And, in this way, I got a friend and a guide in the form of Kanav.'

'So… very soon I will be a nobody because somebody is becoming everybody in your life,' said Shyamli in a bid to tease Param.

'Silly girl! Do you think it can be ever possible?' Param said, holding Shyamli's hand fondly.

Param was narrating her story as if in trance. She said, 'Each day brought us closer, and we are madly in love now. Even his parents seem to like me. His father is a senior army officer, and his mom is actively involved in social work. Even our families bond quite well.'

Shyamli was feeling happy for Param. They hugged and she congratulated her!

By this time Shyamli's parents had reached school. Both the girls sat in the car on its rear seat.

Param kept conversing with Shyamli's mom. 'Aunty and Uncle, my parents will be very happy to meet you. Can I request you to come to our house and have a cup of coffee?'

Shyamli's mom turned back to look towards Paramjeet. She affectionately put her hand on Param's head and said with a smile, 'Sure, my dear, but not now! The city is under so much tension. Moreover, a curfew will be imposed in a few hours' time so it won't be safe at the moment. We will certainly come over to your place once the situation becomes normal to meet your parents.'

Param insisted getting out on the main road because the lane to her house, which was a few steps away from the main road, was thronged by people. Her house was next to the main police station as her father was a senior police officer.

Shamli became a bit concerned. 'Param, why is this crowd near your house?'

Param smiled and said, 'My dear friend, I am quite used to seeing the ocean of people. Whenever there is any law-and-order issue, people line up before the police station. Since the disturbance was in this area, so people must have gathered with complaints, issues, and problems to be redressed.' Shamli breathed a sigh of relief and kissed her friend goodbye.

The traffic on the road was much less than on usual days, but still, the car moved at a slower speed because there were patches of blood on the road through which no vehicle was allowed to pass. The blood-sodden spaces were demarcated with bricks arranged like strings and it allowed much less space for vehicles to pass on the road.

'Wish there was a radio in the car,' Shamli's father said. The technological revolution that we witness today was just a part of fiction movies in those days.

'Yeah, we became so worried after your call from school that we rushed without hearing the midday news, as to what went wrong?' Mom mentioned. 'Thankfully you had taken leave today because of your health issues,' Mom said looking at her father.

And Dad smiled.

As per the report in BBC news, it was a big attack planned by terrorists. They had targeted to kill hundreds of people to pressurize the administration. But the daring police officer and his men managed to foil their attempt, killing a terrorist, and making others run away. And while saving the lives of innocent people, the officer sacrificed his life.

Shamli was hearing news with her family on TV after reaching home. She kept praying for Param's dad's safety.

'This is such a sad state of affairs. These terrorists are real beasts in human form. They all should be hanged!' The angst in Mom's voice reflected on her face, her eyes welled up with tears. The curfew went on for a week with one-hour relaxation every day for people to buy necessary food items.

The next day the state was under the president's rule and the army had taken charge of the city. So, the curfew was removed. Within the environment seething with fear and the feeling of insecurity still lingering in the air, the routine activities, schools and colleges started working.

The morning assembly in the school had an extended session, and there was an announcement of the tragic attack from which they escaped by the skin of their teeth. It was none other than Param's father who bravely fought the terrorists and sacrificed his life. A two-minute silence was observed as a mark of respect for the martyr.

The news made Shamli's head swirl. The news of the killings never appeared as gory as that day. Her heart felt as if it was getting crushed, causing the stream of tears flowing down her cheeks. Shamli wished, if nothing more, she could be at Param's side to be her moral support. But there was strict instruction by the principal that no one was to move out of the school premises, even during break time. Shamli impatiently waited for the classes to end. Since last period was a substitution period, she went to her class teacher to state the problem and the class teacher managed to get her a gate pass and allowed her to visit Param's house.

Shamli was walking down the lane where she had dropped Param. She confirmed the address from a shopkeeper and progressed inside the lane. Walking down the path to Param's house, it felt quite creepy. Maybe the surroundings had taken a cue from the tragic happening and mirrored the sadness.

Shamli attributed this to her prior knowledge of the tragedy that visited Param's family. The lane, which Param said was always full of people, bore a deserted look.

*When the news of the mishap with my friend's family could cause such a jolt, what must Param be undergoing? How will I console her? Has any such word been coined by humans which could reduce the pain of losing loved ones?* Her thoughts skirmished in her mind, and she reached inside the house.

Some people were squatting on the floor carpet in the empty hall area and were sipping tea in small white disposable glasses. The strong current of wind during a hot afternoon wanted to say something to Shamli, which she could not understand. The faces of people did not carry the slightest trace of the tragedy that had visited Param's family. Even during such a painful moment, the folks were enjoying bantering. Seeing her, they pretended to get serious. She sat beside one of them and started enquiring about Param's family. Param's mom was in the hospital due to a severe nervous breakdown.

*Param must be with her mom*, Shyamli thought.

Shyamli realized that there was hardly anything she could do. Then she had to rush back to school fast so as not to miss her vehicle to go back home. *I could wait for Param to come to school and help her in all possible ways*, Shyamli thought and left the place.

But Param did not come to school for days. Shyamli spoke to the school authorities about Param's absence from her house, but no one showed any interest in getting involved in Param's affairs. The power and authority died with the death of her father. There were many giving lip service, but no one was there to help in true spirit.

The central administration managed to bring the situation under control in the state. After years, people breathed peace, but for Shyamli the place could not be the same again. She had a void created due to the absence of Param from her life. After some time, Shyamli's family moved to Delhi as her father got transferred there.

Shyamli's excellent academic record got her a job in her own college as an assistant professor. Her college being a girl's college, there were increasing incidences of eve teasing with the students. She was assigned the duty of meeting the police in charge of the women's cell of the area to report the problem and get suitable arrangements made to ensure the safety of the girls.

Shyamli was made to wait in the meeting room of the police station as the officer in charge was out on a round of sensitive places. Shyamli came to know that the new officer was too tough on hooligans. This was her first posting after her training at the police academy where IPS officers are trained.

After some time, as the officer joined her in the room where Shyamli was waiting both the ladies' jaws dropped and they both froze in their respective places.

The officer rushed and grabbed Shyamli in her arms. Shyamli felt choked and could not utter a word as tears made their way down her cheeks. They both stood hugging each other for a few moments. 'Param, where did you get lost? I had no hopes of meeting you in this life!' Shyamli was uttering words with great difficulty. Shyamli even forgot the reason why she was there.

After the emotional outburst settled, they both sat down and Shamli listened to Param's life story from the day of her father's death.

'Your family dropped me near my house, but I opened my eyes in a dingy place stinking badly. It was the beginning of my miseries. Kanav's family noticed my absence and his father with his contacts in the army got me rescued along with other girls. I stayed with Kanav's family for a few days because Mom had a severe nervous breakdown. After Mom got discharged from the hospital, we had no other place to go to except our village home where my granny stayed with my uncle's family. Our official quarters were taken away from us.'

Param had a let up for her wounds before her dearest friend.

'Mom was not able to recover from her depression, and I was having a terrible time. In her blank eyes, there was no future for us. She would lay in her room the entire day without letting any light seep in. I forcibly fed her a few morsels and the medicines that provided the required energy to her body for the soul to stay in. Uncle's family's behaviour took a complete turn. The days became tougher each day for me to bear. I wondered whether they were the same people who ran from pillar to post to keep father and our family happy whenever we came to spend our holidays at our ancestral house.

'Mom bought beautiful gifts for uncle and his family and even gave them cash before leaving. Now, when we were facing the cruelty of destiny I could see the real and ugly faces of the same relatives who never fail to take credit for whatever they do, which may have been done for their own benefit or free publicity. I was made to slog the whole day doing the household chores. Aunt would keep passing nasty comments for Mom and me, calling us names as witches who took away my father's life. I did not even have the liberty to cry for the fear of depressing the situation further. Despite the odds, I was putting a brave face before the world.

'Our only solace was Granny, the old lady whose wrinkled face and hollow eyes were counting the days left for her heavenly abode. Father's death must have been a bigger shock for her because he was her most prized possession. Dad was her favourite son because he was a caring, dutiful son who not only served his motherland till his last breath, but also was sensitive to the needs of all the family members. Granny held her head high for giving birth to such a son like my father, the likes of him are very rare to find these days. She did not shed even a drop of tears, rather she reduced her food intake which was already limited to single meal in a day. But since that day she started spending more time reading scriptures and reciting on her rosary beads with closed eyes and only her lips and fingers moving agitatedly. She seemed to be strengthening her spiritual being at the cost of her physical existence.

'Uncle and his wife hardly paid heed to Granny's warnings to behave properly with us. I noticed the helplessness on her face whenever Uncle and his family ill-treated us. She would call me near her, at times, and put her pulpy hands on my head. Her frail-looking hand with flesh leaving the bones seemed honed with extraordinary powers due to the spiritual practice of many years, and it made her understand things better despite her reduced visual ability. My trepidation vanished sitting next to Granny and I felt much better in her presence.

'One day uncle slapped me as I slipped holding the tray with food served in costly crockery to some guests waiting in the hall. While I sobbed, Granny gently stood up from the jute woven charpai bed and without asking for any explanation or raising her voice she hit her son hard with her stick saying, 'Enough now! This house belongs as much to my brave son's family as it does to you.'

She asked me to call someone known to us from the city. I instantly though of Kanav's family, and without any further loss of time Granny sent her trusted person to the city with the message. As usual, Kanav's parents came along with the person and helped in all possible ways. With their help, I got admission to a school in Chandigarh, where Kanav was also doing his medicine and a place in the hostel too.

'By the time my father's dues and compensation were cleared, Mom also recovered. She also came to Chandigarh and picked up a job in a school. And, after my studies, I decided to fulfil my father's dream to be a police officer and serve our country. So, this is how you see me here today.'

'And Kanav, where is he?' I asked impatiently.

'Well, he will be finishing his studies at USA in a few months' time and once he is back we will get married. And I am so thankful to God that I have met my bosom buddy before this important day of my life,' Param said with a sparkle in her eyes.

Both the ladies smiled with contentment.

# The Rich Man

The train tore through the thickest and the thinnest sheet of atmosphere, scurrying from one station to another, in the greatest hour of darkness and the hottest hour of the day, roaring with its wildest passion, at its super speed, to reach its destination at the scheduled time. It rocked through rivers, ravines, mountains, and ridges emanating varying sounds, like those of a musical instrument. The yellow velvety mustard fields with mustard flowers in full bloom, and the vast expanse of green and golden wheat fields were a feast for the eyes. Such a picturesque beauty of nature made Pavitra marvel at the unparalleled natural creativity. The train, then, would halt at the station in a city to take a short break, and for the people to board or get off the train. The human voice made the halt at the platform distinguishable – the tea sellers crying their lungs out in their local tongue, *'Chai… chai lelo… garama garam masaledar chai.'* The peanut sellers, and the sellers of local street specialities were pacing to and fro on the platform, from one window to the other of the halting train, like a trained salesman waiting for a second on every window in anticipation of an order.

Pavitra cherished all those sounds, she would try to get the maximum view out of the grilled window and rejoice in its memories later. The happy and sad faces could easily tell the ones waiting to meet their dear ones from those departing from them.

Pavitra's life's journey, from childhood to maidenhood, was linked through innumerable memories of such train journeys, like many of us belonging to the generation born a few decades back; trains being the only means of economical, long-distance travelling.

Pavitra loved train journeys, not because they connected two physical territories which were geographically wide apart, but because both the pieces of land were the dearest locations for her: Punjab and Bihar. The reason was that most of her fond memories had some connection with these places. She, at times, wished the memories to take a physical form as the means of communication, and she could have boarded it to reach her dearest friend in Amritsar.

The train entered the boundaries of Punjab. The land flaunted its economic development; TV antennas mushroomed on the roofs of houses, when television was still considered a luxury in many states of India electronic gadgets had invaded households across all income levels. Tractors could be seen outside most of the houses in the villages; tube wells and water gushing out were also a common sight depicting the economic prosperity of the region.

And, after reaching its destination at Amritsar, the train seemed to look relaxed like a sportsperson relaxing after hearing the declaration of having won a match. Amritsar is the end of Indian territory on the north-western part of the Indian geographical map since India became independent from British rule in 1947. Beyond this area lies Pakistan, created by building a division called Wagah border separating the two independent countries by drawing a line of division on once a common piece of land; like a wall built within a house to separate the living of two closely knit families of brothers.

Some porters in red and white coloured dress had already boarded the train before it came grinding to a halt. The station had an unusually deserted look that day. The men in khaki, the cops, were in the majority at the station.

Pavitra's family descended the train and came out to the main entrance of the railway station to find a transport to drop them home. Strangely, unlike the usual days, there were hardly any cabs and rickshaws in sight at the station.

Pavitra's father walked a few steps away to catch hold of a cab from the nearby area, while the rest of the family waited near the replica of Golden Temple kept in the middle of the entrance to the railway station. Even the miniature form of the replica looked serene and gracious, reminding them of the actual glory of the structure to the devotees. Pavitra had visited the Golden Temple many times with her family. She folded her hand and bowed before the replica, and her mouth watered as she remembered the matchless taste of *karah parshad*, the sacred offering given to devotees after the *darshan* of the sacred shrine.

An old man, with the skin of his face wrinkled into many folds, was leaning on the fluted pillar column along the corner of the entrance, waiting on passengers. He was dressed in an old, ragged kurta, a dark printed *lungi* (an unstitched cloth wrapped around the waist with a knot), a sullied turban and soiled rubber slippers, but his eyes and face shone with some strange kind of glow.

Unlike the normal days, when railway stations used to be thronged by a teeming human population, the station looked calm. There were very few travellers coming out of the train. It was evident that travelling was being avoided by people because of a considerable increase in the killings of innocent people travelling on buses and trains. People resorted to travelling by public transport only in cases of exigencies. It was the time when terrorism was at its peak at Punjab. For Pavitra's family, the summer vacation was the only time when her parents paid a visit to their hometown, and the time for children to meet their doting grandparents.

Despite all odds, the daily wage earners had to move out of their homes for earning a livelihood, but that day even the cabs and autos were missing from the station. So, the *Tonga wala* had his monopoly. Normally, he could hardly manage to get passengers in the city. His clientele was limited to the passengers travelling to nearby villages, who hired the *tonga* because it was cheaper. The takers for the *tonga* – the ancient day chariot pulled by a horse with seats on both sides sharing the same backrest – was decreasing day by day. The traditional and slower means of communication and travel had to bear the brunt of the advancement of technology. The survival of people earning their living through this traditional occupation was becoming difficult.

Tired of travelling for two days in the train, Pavitra's Mom looked worked up. She was looking here and there to catch hold of some vehicle that could be hired to drive them to their home safely. The *Tongawal* rose from his place and came near Pavitra's mom saying in his local tongue, '*Bibi jee aj nai milni koi sawari tuanu, aj ta gadiyan de hartal ha*i,' Madam, you will not get any cab/auto today because of the mass strike and the state-wide protest against the indiscriminate killing of innocent people by terrorists. A big protest march is also likely to begin soon.

The illiterate daily wage earner was trying to woo a passenger so that he could manage a square meal for himself and some fodder for his horse. Probably, he barely had anything to risk, so he was out to earn even amidst the anticipated disturbance. Any activity was of concern for him only to the extent it affected his living.

By that time, Pavitra's father was back, fretting at his futile effort to get the cab. Pavitra's mom, then, shared with him what was told to her by the *Tongawala*. She said, 'Let's hire this tonga otherwise we might miss out on this also.' They had no other option. *Tongawala* could easily read this frustration written on their faces. He started lifting the luggage and adjusting it in the *tonga* even before anyone asked him to do so.

Pavitra's mom lifted her hand to signal him to stop so as to negotiate for the fare, lest they be over charged. Her father could read her mom's mind, and he pressed her hand to stop her from doing that. He murmured, 'You told me that we might not get any cab today then where do you have the choice to negotiate for the fare? We will have to pay whatever amount he asks for, understand?'

'Yes!' Pavitra's mom nodded.

Tongawala had put all the luggage in the tonga and got everyone positioned comfortably. He took the driver's seat. He pulled the reins of the horse and with a light whip the horse started to trot on the empty road, which lacked the hustle and bustle of the normal days. The empty stretch of black pitch grand trunk road showed clearly as there was almost no traffic. The road built by Sher Shah Suri hundreds of years ago still maintained its mark of excellence.

*Tongawala* sang some folk Punjabi songs and even narrated stories about his village. While mentioning Bhangra and the Giddha (the local Punjabi dances) performed at his village, he sang some of the Giddha songs while the horse's trotting sounded like the rhythmic clapping energizing the family, and the tiredness from the long journey vanished to get replaced by a feeling of freshness. The *tongawala* invited Pavitra's family to his village for the Baisakhi festival to witness his son's performance and the spirit of fraternity in the village folks.

With all the talking of Tongawala, the distance of their house was over as if in no time. Tongawala dropped them at their home and helped them in putting the luggage in the house even though Pavitra's family had not solicited it.

On being asked about the fare, tongawala demanded not even a penny more than what was due to him. Pavitra's family was taken with the honesty and civility of the old man. They were so impressed that they gave him double the amount he had asked for. But *Tongawala* kept with him only what he had demanded, and he placed the extra money back in Pavitra's father's hand saying, 'Let me be happy with whatever is due to me. I don't want to get used to getting tips when I am approaching the sunset of my life; it will spoil my habit. I don't want to part with my wealth of contentment by getting used to money which I have not earned.'

The family looked at him with astonishment. A single penny can cause people to be at each other's throats. The whole world is up in arms just for the sake of acquiring material wealth. People are resorting to all means to possess money and wealth, even resorting to unfair practices for minimal material possession, but the man refused what was being gladly offered to him because this meant compromising his values.

Pavitra's parents felt belittled before *Tongawala*. Pavitra's father was telling her mother, 'He has made us rich too with his teaching that the greatest wealth is contentment. It is the treasure that makes one's life happy and peaceful.' They both kept staring at the *Tongawala* moving and fading away from their sight with the sound of trot… trot… trot.

# Jugaad: the innovation

Almost about a decade ago, when the dragon of recession swallowed economies across the globe, India, the so-called, not so robust economy, could break the back of the beast by using *Jugaad*, and survive the turmoil. *Jugaad* is a Hindi colloquial word that refers to an age-old technique in India. The proficiency of Indians in this technique is a gift from their antiquity. It is a science, an art, a tradition, and a philosophy.

Jugaad as per the dictionary means a flexible approach to problem-solving that uses limited resources in an innovative way.

There cannot be an example better than the life of Beni Prasad Bebasia, whose entire life was based on the philosophy of *Jugaad*.

*Jugaad* started playing a role in his life even before his accident of birth. It was after a lot of *jugaads* like going to priests, saints, and worshipping in temples, Beni's parents could have him playing in the corridors of their palatial home. Beni's was a blessed soul, but he was bereft of his share of brain. The portion of intellect in his well-framed body was like a drop in a bucket. But *Jugaad* could compensate for this scarcity so well that Beni's life never felt its shortage.

Beni's parents, exceptionally talented in this age-old technique, could easily embellish Beni's nameplate with high degrees, the prerequisites of a white-collar job and hence, a respectable status in society. Much to the chagrin of his friends, he remained at the top throughout his studies, and the credit for his outstanding performance went to his parents.

Beni's mother was the best friend of his school's principal. So, the examination monster could never intimidate him. Even the formidable board examination was more of a test of Beni's parents' *Jugaad* skills. His super-alert mother did not leave a stone unturned in teaching Beni the basics of this skill. She made sure that he at least learned to copy correctly from the answer slips given by the invigilators, who were already befriended by his family by hook or crook. His mother sat constantly by his side cooling him with a hand-made bamboo fan and feeding him the homemade *desighee ladoos* to keep his mind cool and rejuvenate his dying energy for copying in the exam.

In fact, Beni's father was in greater need of those *ladoos*, because he had been running from pillar to post to find out the addresses of teachers and identify their most cherished needs and desires. This ensured the application of appropriate *Jugaad* for the paper checkers and obtaining the required score to qualify as the top achiever in the exams.

With all the effort and experience of Beni Prasad's father, Beni cleared the first and most important hurdle of the secondary school examination with flying colours. He secured a 1st division. Had Beni's mother diverted her efforts to rejuvenate the energy of Beni's father, instead of Beni, he could have scored yet better and passed with distinction rather than first class.

College education was like a cakewalk because allurements worked more effectively in the case of professors. Each professor provided tuition to the students, and only those students who took tuition from a particular professor were sure to get good marks in his subject. The professor also ensured that the student passed in subsidiary subjects through the contacts he maintained with other professors.

No wonders Beni Prasad managed to get highest marks in all subjects because of the blessings of goddess Lakshmi on his family. Every stage of Beni's education was funded by selling a piece of land. Both his parents had inherited huge landed properties from their ancestors. Beni's parents thought that there could not be a better use of their huge inheritance than to brighten the future of their son and make him a part of shining India. Beni's parents' dreams became live when the two high-sounding degrees MA and an LLB, suffixed his name. A big silver nameplate with his degrees embossed in golden letters was mounted outside the gigantic entrance gate of their house.

Finally, Beni Prasad's status changed to Shri Bebasia ji, from triple B to single B with a high sounding prefix

*Shri* and a suffix *ji* like every stage of enhancement in a technological gadget makes it functionally more efficient and smaller in terms of its physical size.

Shri Bebasia became a lecturer in the college from where he obtained his degrees. Contending for the only post of the lecturer was quite easy because his marks were more than all the other applicants. Beni had everything needed to lead a happy and comfortable life. But for his parents, an important event that needed completion before passing over the maintenance of the clan's ownership was his marriage to a girl from a reputable family. It was time to search for a proposal with a fine toothcomb.

While Beni's mother was exploring the proposal of prospective brides for her son, Beni's heart fell for Bela.

It so happened that some of Beni's friends, who had left the small town to pursue higher education in the capital city of Delhi, planned a study tour of their town with a few friends. They contacted Beni for their stay arrangements and Beni showed his magnanimity by arranging for their stay in his huge guest house. It was a group of three boys and two girls: Nalin, Suraj, Vikram, Parul and Bela.

Nalin and Suraj were Beni's childhood friends. They came with their three city friends making a total of five. Out of the two ladies, one was Nalin's fiancée Parul. Bela was Parul's sister who joined her sister's friends for a fun trip to the town after bagging a plush job with a computer company that she managed after her degree as a software engineer.

When Beni was welcoming his friends at the railway station he was struck by the beautiful face of Bela, and his eyes recorded her every little gesture into his mind's video reel. Her long silky hair swaying with her swagger on her high heels, loose top and tight pants. Her cheerful, pretty face with innocent eyes made Beni fall for her head over heels. Bela stoked up his dormant yearnings for a life partner. He had his desires mounting like the high tide waves on a full moon night.

He decided to get married to Bela. But, alas, this time the old age technique did not come in handy. There was no way to win Bela's heart other than to approach her through Parul.

Well, Beni too had impressed Bela with his athletic body and the strict fitness regime he followed. His other qualifications were his simple manners and a huge inheritance, and all these traits qualified him as the most eligible bachelor for the damsels of his town, but for Bela there was a lot that needed to be done by Beni before being chosen as a life partner by her. She was a career-oriented girl from a big city and for her, job was an important ingredient for the recipe for happiness. Bela was not ready to sacrifice her career for Beni. So, her condition for marrying Beni was that he would have to shift his base to the city where Bela lived. But, despite trying all the jugaad he could not manage a job in the city.

And, finally, he had to settle for a wife chosen by his parents. Her name was Shalu. It was difficult for Shalu, a shy and diffident girl who was the complete opposite of

Bela, to woo Beni initially. But Beni's soft heart could not remain immune to the genuine care and unconditional love of his wife. One day when he returned late at night after spending time with his friends at the hotel, his eyes fell on Shalu's dusky face, who had dozed off sitting on the floor with her head resting on the bed, and found some magnetic attraction in it. Shalu woke up with the noise of Beni entering the room, and her sleepy, innocent eyes were irresistible.

Beni started living happily with his wife and the news of his wife becoming pregnant brought in greater moments of happiness for the entire family.

After the night-long drizzling, the weather in the early morning was pleasant. Amidst heavy downpours, the clear sky was a rarity. Like the unwanted guests whose needless and untimely presence spoils the day to day routine of the house, the rains came unannounced and continued without interruptions, the temperament of nature remained highly unpredictable.

Shalu was in endless labour pain, in a small dark room, along with the traditional midwife, Bedamia, as she was known in the town. Bedamia was well known for her prowess at relieving ladies from their pain and making them deliver healthy babies with ease. There was no qualified gynaecologist in the town. Bedamia alone handled all the delivery cases there.

Shalu was begging Bedamia, 'Please ask my husband to call my parents.'

Bedamia tried to console Shalu saying, 'Don't worry, things will soon be all right.' A few moments later the husky voice of Bedamis filled the verandah. 'Baby is born!' The next sentence that, 'A baby girl is born,' filled the environment with silence, but the news of Shalu's death filled the air with gloom and sadness. The baby was handed to Beni's mother. Bedamia accepted her fault that Shalu should have been taken to a hospital in the city where better treatment could have saved Shalu's life. Application of jugaad in areas where vital decisions are involved can be detrimental.

The baby's enchanting face moved Beni deeply. He looked at her with tearful eyes and took a pledge in his heart that he would educate his daughter to become a doctor and this time he would teach her to follow the proper long route to success because one can use jugaad for meeting the needs of life with limited resources, but the resource of hard work that has been given to humans should be used to the fullest to achieve one's dreams and the success in life. The success managed through jugaad would fail when it is needed the most.

# The Gold Chain

Suraj decided to take a half day off from the office. Life, to date, had been like that on a highway; racing at the maximum speed, throwing caution to the winds, full of thrill, excitement, and fun. But suddenly everything started appearing meaningless. His desires and dreams were all fulfilled, then what more he could he want? His mind raised this question. And the heart squelched. It was like, he was crossing paths with his own self.

Suraj could not enforce his will on his senses any more. His head throbbed badly, and he wanted to take a break, a break from the rut, the daily routine. He wanted his headache to settle before proceeding home, but it didn't. He applied some pressure by holding his head firmly between both his hands, but that didn't help either.

And finally, he popped in a painkiller and left for home. While driving, his mind started calculating the number of days after which he was taking a break. As he recounted, the activities were lined up in tandem, and it made him reach the day he landed on his dreamland, the *terra firma* of the United States of America. Young brains from across the globe came to this land to turn their dreams into reality.

Thankfully, it was on a Friday that his consciousness revolted against his physical body, and the following two days were weekend holidays. And a weekend with no meetings and appointments was of a very rare kind. He was feeling a bit lighter by the time he was home.

Suraj parked his car and rushed towards the door to open its lock. While doing this, he paused for a moment to look around at the surroundings in absolute peace, in broad day sunlight. His gaze got riveted by the wooden mailbox bearing a wearied look. It had lost most of the lustre of its new paint. It clung to the external surface of the shining white wall of his house like a plebeian amidst a gathering of noblemen. Suraj thought he would get some paint for the mailbox and get its new look back. Forcing a smile to evade feeling guilty, he switched his mind to the thought of fetching the keys of the mailbox.

But was his feeling justified? Weren't the mailboxes a redundant item in modern houses? He was engaging in logic with his mind. He muttered to himself, 'To expect postal mail is foolishness in the age of the computer revolution. And I can bet there would be no mail in the box.' He was turning the key to unlock the box while his mind kept arguing: *Proof of the pudding in is eating, and if there is no mail, I shall get this box removed, but I need to at least check before taking any decision*. And the moment the box door was ajar, some envelopes slipped from the box to the floor. There was a good number of envelopes inside the letter box that rejected his decision to remove the mailbox. He apologetically lifted his eyes to look towards the box, which stared in his eyes with all the beautiful memories associated with it.

Before getting married to Tanya, he used to check the mailbox daily; rather, he impatiently waited for Tanya's handmade cards and letters doused in the sweet smelling fragrance of his favourite perfume. Tanya chose postal mail over the internet to send him love messages. She said, 'Reading a message in hard copy has a more lasting impression, and preserving those memories is also easy.' After taking out all letters he affectionately moved his hand over the box with an assurance that it was irreplaceable.

He carried the letters inside and put them on his study table. Tanya was still not back from her pre-natal maternity classes. It was her ninth month of pregnancy. Both Suraj and Tanya were waiting for their baby with bated breath. They had been living their dreams with a child who did not yet land in this world.

*Why am I feeling so uneasy today?* Suraj thought. He confirmed with Tanya and she said that everything was fine. Then, why was the feeling that something was amiss?

With a hot cup of coffee, he placed himself in a comfortable posture on the couch and threw the entire bunch of letters next to him. He threw a cursory glance at the bunch of envelopes and could identify the letters from India by the Indian postal stamp, and some he instantly identified with the handwriting in which the address was marked. With his free hand he took out all his letters from India and put them for priority reading, and with the other, he sipped his hot coffee. As he lifted one letter and brought it near to his eyes, it was like a complete show becoming live on an electronic gadget gone dead. His fondest memory flashed back within seconds which he had almost forgotten. Those were letters from his mother from India.

There was a total of four letters. The three were in his mother's handwriting, but he did not have any clue regarding the handwriting on the fourth letter. *Well, let me first read Amma's letters*, he thought.

He tore open the first letter. It was written in a happy tone in which Amma had expressed joy at Tanya's pregnancy. Suraj remembered that he had last spoken to his mother to convey to her that Tanya was pregnant. And the words of blessings still echoed in his ears.

His mind started being flooded with old memories, his childhood day in a small town in India. Suraj remembered how Amma had looked after him and his grandmother after the death of Babujee, his father. She alone shouldered all the expense of his education and Grandma's medical costs. She had sold off all her valuables for his higher education. But he was a failure as a son, because he did not fulfil any responsibility as a son. He was full of remorse.

All her three letters had the same question: *Suraj when will you visit India?* But the third letter read quite depressingly.

*Suraj,*

*I don't know for how long I will stay in this world. Before my final goodbye, I want to have a glimpse of you with your wife.*
*Amma.*

After reading the letter, he was choked with emotions, and tears welled up in his eyes. He was cursing his super successful life in America which made him overlook an important corner of his heart.

With a heavy heart, he picked up the last letter from India. And by the time the contents of the letter were in front of him, he was up in action. Within seconds he had already headed towards the telephone.

He called up his secretary to book him a ticket to India on the next available flight. And, by the time Tanya was back, Suraj had made all his preparations to leave for India, the next day.

Tanya looked a bit perplexed at Suraj's decision. 'What happened, Suraj?' she asked.

Suraj showed her the letter that his mother was ill, but Tanya was unable to buy his idea of leaving for India in such a rush, leaving his pregnant wife behind. She said, 'You can send her some money and ask her to get checked up by a good doctor, that's it. Why is there a need of such hullabaloo?'

'Tanya will you please shut up!' Suraj said. 'You very well know that I am leaving you behind with enough support system to look after you in my absence. I have asked Pam and Harry to come and stay with you. And in any case I will be back after four days. It has been years since I met my mother, and you are stopping me even after knowing that she is critically ill.'

Tanya was very upset with Suraj; stamping her foot angrily she left for her bedroom speaking at the top of her lungs. 'Suraj, staying in America has not changed you a wee bit! You remain that typical Indian emotional fool.'

Suraj was looking at his house from some distance, the forlorn house. Long blades of wild vegetation had hidden it from a clear view from outside. The brick boundary was covered with a sheet of green and brown algae. A few bricks had broken from the centre of the boundary wall, and the portion of the wall visible from some distance had *BABA CHAAP ZARDA*, the advertisement of the best selling tobacco company in the city.

Suraj's feet stuck to the land. He wished *Amma* to come out and wrap him in her arms. While his gaze was still fixed on the entrance to his house, he felt a soft hand touching his shoulder from behind. He turned his face to look at the person who had kept his hand on him. It was *Shambhu Chacha*, Suraj's father's best friend and their immediate neighbour.

Before Suraj could say anything *Shambhu chacha* held him by the side of his arms and led him towards his house which was just a few steps away from Suraj's house.

'How are you, Suraj? Did you receive my letter?'

Suraj nodded. 'Yes, *chacha*! Where is *Amma*?'

'*Amma* kept waiting for you, Suraj, but her body did not support her. She left us forever.'

Suraj almost froze on the land where he was sitting.

*Shambhu Chacha* was speaking in a grieved voice. 'There are very few ladies like your mother, *Suraj*. She bore all pain herself, but she did not share even a trace of her problems with you. She ensured celebrating every happy occasion of your life with all the fervour she could afford and continued showering her blessings on you.'

'She had started taking tuition the past few months. Despite her failing health, she didn't stop. I and my wife kept insisting that she should join you in the USA. I assured her of making all the preparations too, but she made an excuse that she cannot go and stay anywhere else except her home. She used to say that when Suraj will come with his wife and baby, she would organize a grand celebration. And she would go to you only when your baby is born so that she could spend time with the child. With the onset of winter, her health started deteriorating. One day she had a severe attack of asthma. *Ramu*, your servant, was knocking frantically at our door. I took out my car, and I and my wife rushed her immediately to the hospital. But, alas, we could not save her. Even before reaching the hospital, she breathed her last. And I didn't want you to get disturbed by the news, so had mentioned that she was critically ill.'

By that time *Sharda*, *Shambhu chacha*'s wife, had also joined them.

She said, 'Suraj, my son, *Padma*, your mother, entrusted me with a responsibility before saying her final goodbye to this world.' Saying this, she handed a packet to Suraj. She further added, 'Padma was confident that you will come to see her after the birth of your baby. She had asked me to keep this packet safely and hand it to you when you come to India.'

Suraj took the packet with tearful eyes. He started to open the packet when *Shambhu chacha* added, '*Suraj*, don't open the packet in front of us. Open it when you are with your family.'

Suraj said, '*Chacha*, you people have been more than family to us.' While saying this he looked towards *Shambhu Chacha*'s wife, with sad eyes.

Suraj opened the packet, fold after fold, layer after layer, to reveal its contents. There were some of the clothes of his early childhood days, the discoloured woollen baby set. At the end of every winter *Amma* used to put all woollen clothes in the sun, for drying all moisture, before packing them away for use in the forthcoming winters, and she would fondly hold the baby woollen set in her hands and become lost in memories. That baby set was prepared by Suraj's grandmother before his birth, and she preserved it with the utmost care. This set reminded her of the days of her pregnancy. *Amma* always used to say that she would knit beautiful sweaters and baby sets for her grandchild.

Beneath the old baby set, there were two more new woollen sets that Amma had knitted. Suraj picked up each piece, the baby cap, the small socks, the sweater and gazed at each of them, bringing them close to his eyes, and broke down bitterly.

He calmed himself and lifted the red silk pouch which was safely placed within those woollen clothes. The pouch looked very beautiful. It was made of pure silk cloth with a thick red silk thread passing through the hole that ran the entire length of the pouch. The pouch was tied with a knot in the thread with the name "Shantilal jeweller" embroidered with white thread. Suraj opened the knot and pulled the opening apart to widen the gap to find something sparkling inside. There was a gold chain with a small pendant of Lord *Ganesha* dangling on the chain.

Seeing the gold chain both *Shambhu chacha* and his wife looked at each other. *Shambhu chacha* said, 'So this was the gift for which *Bhabhi* had started taking extra tuitions despite her bad health. Whenever we asked her the reason for exerting so much, she would say, "*Shabhujee* you will soon come to know about the reason".'

Suraj brought the packet near his closed eyes and kissed it as if it was his mother. He cried bitterly once more. His heart felt like exploding and getting pounded to pieces.

Suraj sat in the ambulance along with Tanya. Her waters had broken and she was being rushed to the hospital, in an emergency. After a few hours of surgery, Tanya delivered a baby boy, but the baby had died in the womb.

Suraj's heart wrenched with grief. He sat beside Tanya on the hospital bed. Tanya had a blank expression on her face. She was listlessly looking at the wall clock. She did not look at Suraj, even once.

Suraj, with his heart broken, was not finding suitable words to break the ice. He held Tanya's hand between both his hands. Tanya's face looked repentant. Tears were flowing down from the corner of her eyes. Without turning her gaze towards him Tanya spoke. 'Suraj, God wanted me to understand and feel the love of a mother for her child before giving me my child in my arms. Now I can feel the pain your Amma must have felt for you when you were not with her. The craving of a mother for her child; I can understand a bit too late.' She folded her hands and looked up towards the roof of the room and begged, 'I'm sorry, *Amma*! Please forgive me!'

Suraj's lips trembled. The feelings crossed all boundaries, and he covered his face with his own hands. Tears flooded his face again. There was deluge of tears on Tanya's face too. Both wanted to ameliorate their heart's pain with water from tears.

A little while later, when Suraj regained his composure, he remembered the gold chain which he had been carrying with him from the time he was back from India. He took out the gold chain and put it in Tanya's hand saying, 'Tanya, we will keep *Amma*'s blessing for our next child.' Both looked at each other trying to search for some leftover dream in the other's eye.

# Beauty is only skin deep

I geared up for the first day of my college with my heart bouncing like a ping- pong ball. It felt like having taken an independent flight to the world of newfound freedom. Yes! I was at my destination! My feet stood firm on the floor of the most prestigious college in our city. There were guys and gals, all new admissions like me, out of the regime of the strict code of conduct at schools. Freedom was in the air, and we rejoiced in. every bit of it.

The college was famous for all the right reasons; great infrastructure, intake of the cream from the student population, and the most important being its "bower of bliss" colloquially called "Majnu ka tilla". The place took its name from Majnu, the legendary hero of Laila, Majnu, the eternal lovers. Though the fact is not historically supported, the name was acquired in the sense the place was made use of.

The slightly elevated area made beautiful with verdant patches and plenty of trees surrounding it was the most desired location for *love birds*. It was mainly the fresher boys and girls formed into couples sitting together, arm in arm, and looking ecstatic. The place was singled out by young hearts for their much fantasized dalliance with their sweethearts, the desire for whom had begun after they stepped into puberty but was taking shape after their safe landing in the college.

The eyes played the role of a judge in making the selection of a partner. The guys and gals decked out in branded clothes, driving a swanky car, and walking with a swagger formed into pairs within no time. People like me were second in line, on the lookout for someone suitable to pair with. Being from a middle-class background was our biggest drawback.

Tilla was smack in the middle of the college building and the canteen. Every day I walked many times from my class to the canteen and had to pass through Majnu ka tilla. I envied couples romancing, lost in looking in each other's eye as if they were surfing in ocean of love.

I sat in the canteen, wool-gathering, while sipping from a hot cup of coffee. My desire to woo a boyfriend was being further nourished by the delay. Thinking that the effort in this direction was like a wild goose chase, I decided to shift my focus towards studies, the real reason for being in college. So, I decided to pay a visit to the library.

I walked into the library for the first time after joining the college. Since I just wanted to bide my time, I picked up a fashion magazine from the magazine stand placed right at the entrance and comfortably got seated on a chair closest to the air conditioner, feeling much better on getting a full blast of cool air directly on my face. I apathetically investigated the magazine pages while fighting a battle with the airflow to hold the pages in readable position.

'Excuse me!'

The voice tore my attention from my thoughts with which I was deeply engrossed, and I turned my head to look straight at the point of its origin.

'I am talking to you!'

A guy seemed to have appeared from the woodwork, and he was addressing me. The moment my glance fell on his face, I got exasperated not only because he was a stranger, but also because of his looks. Long unkempt hair, untrimmed beard, and sleepy eyes looking from behind his thick glasses made him look creepy. He was holding a pile of books in his hand and stood right behind my chair.

I flew off the handle and curtly asked, 'What's the matter?'

But he still maintained his cool and said politely, 'Can you please vacate my seat?'

'Your seat! I mean, do we have to reserve our seat in the library?' I asked scornfully. There were very few students in there, and those of them who were, looked at us with raised eyebrows.

He looked baffled. Seeming to be in no mood to pick up fight, he said, 'Okay! Please let me pick up my notebook and the pen so that I can take another seat.'

I looked at the table in front of me, which I failed to notice earlier, and there I spotted the notebook and a pen with its cover fixed on its hind side.

I sat there dumbstruck, unable to decide about my next action. In the meantime, he lifted his notebook and pen kept in front of me on the table and placed it above the pile of books he was holding, and moved away quietly. His genteel manners betrayed his looks.

With the load of books in his hands, he settled on the nearest available seat. The place was in the middle of all disturbances. It fell along the main passage of the library through which students came in and went out; even the air from the AC hardly reached there. The seat was diagonally opposite to where I was seated, but two rows away in between.

Unconsciously, my eyes got lifted to check the expressions on his face, as I presumed that he must be fretting at me because of the scuffle, but I found his gaze fixed on me. I instantly bent my head to save my sneak peek from being caught. I had begun to feel restless and decided to leave instantly.

I got acclimatized to the surroundings and befriended some of the swankiest guys in the college. The bonhomie with anyone among them could not last longer than a month because it was difficult for me to meet their expectations and demands which were not in accordance with my family values.

By the time a few months passed, it was time for students to be back to the salt mines. The examination time was right around the corner. It was time for the reality check, and then the realization dawned that I had wasted all my time on futile activities.

In a bid to be classified as modern and sassy, I had made a complete mess of my studies. Since I had bunked classes, I did not even have class notes. It was like my chickens had come home to roost and I did not know where to look up for help. All my friends with whom I had walked hand in hand on Majnu ka tilla managed to buy notes from professors by burning holes in their pockets. I knew none of them who had been promising to bring stars for me would be ready to even share the notes with me.

Totally confounded, I moved into the library. Carrying tons of worries and loads of pain in my heart, I was in the library, for the second time since I joined the college. I randomly selected some books from the aisle and took a seat which first fell my way. I wished I could get hold of some magic band to make me pass my examinations with flying colours, but the magic happens only in imagination, not in real life.

And again, my attention was disturbed by a voice calling out right from next to me. It was the same young man with whom I had picked up a fight earlier for the seat. His eyes were fixed on my face with a question in his eyes. He seemed to have read all the worries lingering in my mind.

'Hello... Excuse me... What's the problem?'

The moment I looked at his face, I felt my ears burning with guilt and embarrassment, and I couldn't utter a word.

But he looked pretty cool, with no hard feelings at all. I said, 'No! Nothing! I'm fine!'

He looked at me with a smile and said, 'Ms Mallika, I am your senior and we are in for the same course, economics honours.'

My eyes fixed on his face; I was gobsmacked.

He knew so much about me, and I had been thinking of him as a stranger for all this while.

'Don't be surprised as to how I know so much about you. On the freshers' party day, all you freshers introduced yourselves, and I being the final year student was part of the audience,' he said, seeming to have read my mind so well.

Having gained back my confidence, I looked at him with a feeling of penitence and said, 'Yes, you are right!' By this time, I was totally overwhelmed with the young man and felt quite comfortable in his company.

The warmth and sincerity in his words made my apprehensions vanish, and in a choked voice, I shared all the foolishness I was up to since the time I had joined college. Being sure that I would flunk my exams, I started sobbing.

He comforted me saying, 'It's good that there is still a little time for the exams to begin. I have all the notes from the first year preserved with me. I shall bring them for you. Still, in case of any problem, you can ask me to explain to you.' And he decided to give me free coaching for an hour every day in the college, before the exams.

And this offer raised my hopes, giving a lift to my sagging confidence. I started to raise myself up from the chair, asking, 'Okay, at what time shall I come to the library tomorrow?'

He said, 'Not here! Didn't you notice the number of students in the library today?' I looked around and saw that there was good growth in the number of new faces in the library, as compared to the other day. He said, 'As the examination days draw nearer, you will find more crowds shifting to the library.'

'Then?'

Before I could further add he said, 'Come to the canteen and from there we will go to Tilla which will remain deserted during examination days because the students will throng the library now.'

And then I realized that I didn't even know his name till then, because I never bothered to give a damn about a person who was not good to look at. Having read my mind again, he said, 'If you are not able to locate me at the canteen then ask someone for Aniket. If I'm late for any reason then wait for me for a few minutes, and I'll be there.'

The next day, I was at the canteen at the scheduled time, but Aniket was still to arrive. I went to enquire about him from the person on the cash counter, who was being addressed as Veerji. Veerji asked me to wait for ten to fifteen minutes. Probably, Aniket informed him about the expected delay.

No sooner did I occupy a seat, a young boy came with a tray lined with a red cloth with a cup of coffee and a plate with colourful macaroons. I looked at the boy with surprise. I said, 'I don't need anything. Thanks.'

But the boy placed every item, one by one, on the table and said, 'Aniket sir's guest is our guest,' and he narrated all information about Aniket within minutes.

Aniket belonged to an affluent business family, but the business never interested him. He had his heart set on his studies. After faring well in intermediate exams, he could manage a seat with the scholarship in this college. Despite all his riches, he didn't take a penny from his parents. From his scholarship money, he even managed to save some to help the needy. Many times, he gave money to Chandu and helped other helper boys in the canteen in times of need.

Chandu's description of Aniket's larger than life image was impacting me deep down. The more I came to know about Aniket, the better was becoming my perception of human personality and behaviour.

With Aniket's help in the nick of time, I felt quite confident to take the exams, and had my hopes raised to clear my papers with flying colours.

On the result declaration day, I waited amidst the crowd of students packed like sardines in front of the noticeboard where the result was displayed, to find out about their performance in the exams. I had planned to meet Aniket after seeing my result.

By this time, I had come to know a lot about Aniket, and that all through he had been the university's top achiever in economics. After a lot of struggling, I could manage to look at the list and was relieved to see my name finding a mention in the list of students passing with a first class. *No need to check Aniket's result. Like all other years, he only will be the top this time too.* Then I would have to wait and struggle for another half an hour to reach the point from where I could look at the list to know his marks, that I was sure Aniket must have already found out for himself. With these thoughts I moved on towards the canteen to meet Aniket and thank him for all he had done for me.

While walking towards the canteen with racing steps, I threw a quick glance at the Tilla and remembered the dedication with which Aniket tutored me. Along with academic learning, he also taught me the greatest lesson of life, that one should never be judgmental. Beauty in the true sense is about how beautiful one is as a person, or one's inner personality. I just wanted to go to the Tilla and shout at the top of my voice that Aniket was the most handsome man in the college.

I reached the canteen and went to Veerji at the counter to enquire about Aniket. Veerji kept attending to customers and seemed to ignore me. I looked around for Chandu, thinking him to be the best person who could tell me about Aniket, but even he was not around. I repeated my question a couple of times then Veerji finally obliged. He locked his cash drawer and signalled me to come aside.

He said, 'Mallikajee what kind of friend you are! You didn't even try to know how and where your friend had been for all these days?'

'Why? What happened?' I asked narrowing my eyes.

'Aniket is in hospital and Chandu is with him assisting his family in taking care of Aniket,' Veerji said.

My mouth was agape; I could not even ask what happened. Veerji started narrating the incident:

'Before the examinations, the demand for tea, coffee and cigarettes increased from the hostel. Chandu and the other canteen boys had to go the extra mile in making deliveries to students. On one unfortunate night, Chandu went to deliver orders for tea at some point at midnight, in a room adjacent to Aniket's. Chandu had to do double duty that day and he had requested me to allow him to leave after that order. But the boys placed an order for a particular brand of cigarette to be fetched from the market. Some of the boys were drunk like fish and they needed cigarettes desperately. The market had closed by that time, and Chandu came back empty handed much to the chagrin of the boys. One of the boys slapped him for not being able to fulfil their demands. The yelling and commotion made Aniket and the boys from nearby rooms come out. Aniket could not tolerate Chandu being beaten up badly by the boys. He intervened and the fight became furious. Aniket was the only one fighting for Chandu and the rest all joined to beat Aniket up. Chandu, somehow, managed to come back to the canteen and call me. I, along with my staff, went to the spot and somehow rescued Aniket. The ruffians had beaten Aniket very badly. We immediately rushed Aniket to the nearest hospital so he could get medical aid to prevent the beatings becoming fatal. Aniket suffered multiple fractures and was still recovering in the hospital.

I have left Chandu in the hospital so that he can assist Aniket's family to run errands.'

After hearing all this, I could not wait for an extra second and rushed to the hospital to meet Aniket. Aniket had recovered quite a bit, but was still unable to walk without the crutches. His face was undistinguishable due to multiple bandages covering his wounds. Seeing me, his lips curved into a smile and he asked, 'How are you, Mallika?'

Tears rolled out of my eyes. I went near him and held his hand, and instead of replying, I said, 'How could they beat you like beasts? I am going to write a complaint against them.'

Chandu replied, 'Ma'am, the culprits are behind bars now. Veerji phoned the college principal on that very day and the principal immediately called the police to take action against all the students who were involved in the beating. There were six of them and all six have also been expelled from the college.'

When Chandu named the six of them my head hung in shame because, with two of them from the gang, I had spent time on Majnu ka tilla. They both looked suave and belonged to rich and influential families.

But Aniket also had good news to share. He had his admission confirmed in a few of the best foreign universities with a full scholarship. And the college would assess him for the final year based on his past record because the mark sheet was required for the final formalities before admission in universities.

So many things had happened, and I had clues of nothing; but how could have I been aware of things when I was relaxing after the exams? But from that day onwards till Aniket was discharged from the hospital I remained with him for the entire day.

One day Aniket invited me for a cup of coffee in the college canteen.

All that I had wished was coming true, and I sat with my dream mate enjoying every sip of coffee with the name and face put on the handsome person I dreamt of being with. And then it was me who asked for the favour. 'Can we sit together on Tilla for a while?'

Aniket smiled. We held each other's hands and our eyes surfed in the ocean of love in our partner's eyes. Aniket popped the question to which I had to say yes because I had got the most handsome person in my life about whom I had been dreaming all the while.

# Truly yours

I was sitting in the plane ready for take-off. After three years of continuous stay in a foreign land, my eyes starved to have a look of my own land, my motherland. My ears ached to listen to melodious tunes of local songs sung by my granny, and the ladies singing the chorus to her songs. I had taken leave for a complete month. I knew very well that even this one-month period would not be enough, keeping in view the amount of work to be accomplished.

Mom had already sent me the blueprint of her plans. My cousin's marriage at Muzaffarpur was at top of the list. Muzaffarpur, my ancestral hometown, was our most favourite holiday destination during the summer vacations at school. The thoughts of Muzaffarpur struck a chord and nostalgia gripped my contemplations. I was becoming impatient to be at Muzaffarpur to check whether the leftover stones of mangoes we consumed, which I used to plant by digging and covering them with earth, had developed roots and grown into trees or not.

As the plane made its way through the smoky clouds, my imagination took flight to my childhood days. The soothing memories spilled over my stressed mind and I felt cool and cheerful. I was reliving every bit of the memory

– right from the preparations to go to Muzaffarpur. The groundwork for the journey started much ahead of our summer vacation: the buying of gifts, the train reservations etcetera. Mom used to buy gifts not only for her relatives, but also for her neighbours, servants and mementoes for some accounted souls who happened to pay a visit during our stay at Muzaffarpur.

As a child, with no responsibility of duties, the entire journey was a fun trip for us, as those were the days when there were no shopping malls and multiplexes and we looked forward to travelling to our grandparents' place for all the pampering and fun.

Muzaffarpur was not connected through the main line junction so express trains ended at Patna, the state capital city. We had to board a steamer after an overnight train journey to Patna. Travel by steam ship was much more entertaining than the journey by train.

I clung to the steamer railing at its periphery, looking at the waves of water forming below, as it raced over it. The steamer ripped up the water to move ahead. I used to get lost watching the meandering river, surging up and down, along with the steamer. Mom would buy salt and black pepper sprinkled hot boiled egg from the boys boiling eggs on a movable metal furnace, and selling to the passengers. She joined me near the ship railing to enjoy the sight of the river waves, and feed me my favourite hot boiled eggs. I still relish the taste of those eggs which tasted very different from the ones boiled by mom at home.

I could well remember Grandma bursting into tears and hugging Mom passionately on seeing us after a long time; the same way Mom does after I reach home from USA.

I calculated the number of gifts that I had bought as per the list sent by Mom, and felt relaxed that I could buy everything that she wanted. There was a wrist watch for *Saryu kaka* and a leather jacket for his son *Ram Chander*, which I bought of my own accord. *Saryu kaka* occupies an important place in my memory because he made my childhood days very special.

He used to give me a ride to all the places I wished to go to, as I was strictly prohibited by G to go to certain areas except in the company of a grown-up person. The rainy season at Granny's place always coincided with our school vacations and I loved to see the nature having freshened up after rains; like the feel of freshness after a cool refreshing bath. The roads used to be clogged with water and the innumerable pot holes on them were barely visible because of water logging. Saryu kaka would take the short cut and ride his cycle through the fields along the railway tract.

It used to be early in the morning when *Saryu kaka's* duty was to fetch vegetable fresh from the farm before the farmers took it to the market for selling. This was the time when the labourers (men and women) who had come to work on the new factory project and staying in the makeshift camps, attended to their natural call, in the lush green surrounding along the railway tract. I covered up my eyes such as to avoid seeing them. I used to bend my head and my eyes would dig into the ground below to enjoy the variegated coloured pedestrian brick path covered with algae. For Saryu kaka the ride through the path was of special delight.

As the gusts of wind vibrated trees, water collected on their leaves dropped off on us, and tickled me to an excited shriek. People hiding behind the bushes were exposed to the naked gaze of passersby. As the trees moved with the wind, Saryu kaka could steal glances at some pretty young girls collecting branches and tree twigs for the fuel. Saryu kaka would wink at those girls with a naughty whistle and a smile, and the girls responded by covering their faces with their dupattas. It used to be a typical scene from a Bollywood movie. Saryu kaka tied the knot with one of those girls, and was blessed with his son Ram Chander.

Saryu Kaka used to take pride in introducing me to all his friends and acquaintances as I was his *Maalik* (master's) grandson, and my being with him depicted the trust of his master which he commanded. The cycle, which he loved not less than I love my Audi that I bought with my first salary, was gifted by Grandpa. Saryu kaka applied brakes on his cycle, and my eyes opened with the air hostess making an announcement that the plane had reached Indira Gandhi International Airport.

It was after many years that all the members of our extended family were gathering for the marriage celebration. It was the marriage of my uncle's daughter

Revati. Everyone in the family was quite excited about the get together at the grandparents' home.

Revati and her prospective groom both worked in Singapore, but *Mamu* (uncle) thought this occasion was an opportunity for the family get together, in the luxury of the huge bungalow with a fruit orchard in the backyard and a beautiful garden at the door entrance. The grandparents were very happy with this decision of Uncle, and so were the other members of the family.

The grandparents became busy in renovating the old house to give it the look of a bride; a complete makeover with new emulsion paint and minor repairs. The gusto was in the air. After a long time, there was going to be a reunion of families. When we were kids, it happened every year, but now after nearly ten years all uncles and aunts were collecting at the grandparents' house to attend the marriage.

Age stole some firmness from the bodies of *Nani* (Granny) *and Nana* (Grandpa), but the warmth of their affection was same rather more because all their children were coming together after a decade. Their eyes sparkled with happiness. Servants too had grown old, including Saryu kaka. His son Ram Chander took charge of running errands.

Ram Chander said while touching Mom's feet, 'Cheeru bhaiya, your mango tree has blossomed into a big tree. It also bears fruits in every season.'

Before I could ask him more about the tree, Grandma said, 'Chandu, go and get tea for everyone. You can do all the talking later.' As he left Granny said in her monologue, 'Given an opportunity he can talk endlessly for the entire day. That's why I need to be a bit strict with him. He is just not like his father.'

I too felt a bit tired, and moved away smilingly into my room to freshen up. But *Chandu's* mention of the mango tree brought the throwback memory alive when me and Poornima used to play for the entire day in the garden, and once we sowed some stones of mangoes into the soil in our fruit orchard. I gave instructions to *Saryu Kaka* to look after it in my absence, and that he had been doing religiously; that was why even Chandu knew about it.

Away from my soil, I was tired of the slog of life, and this place was having a tranquilizing effect on my mind. There was no change in the room setting from what it was when I was a child. I was inspecting every item kept in the room – the big steel trunks covered with cross stitch embroidered covers done by Granny. The wooden almirah with old books and diaries stacked in it. I took out a diary that looked quite familiar and flipped through its pages. It was Babli aunty's diary where she had her secret messages drafted for her boyfriend she admired in her college. With the flashback of memories, I was rolling on the floor laughing seeing the scribbling done on aunt's notes, and some missing pages from in between the diary. I made paper boat to float them in the pool of rainwater in the potholes of our big lawn. I still remember, how Mom shouted at me when aunt complained to her that I tore off some important pages of her diary. Instead of me, Babli aunty got a scolding from Grandpa that she did not keep her things properly. After all, how could someone speak anything against his *ladla*, i.e favourite grandson. Babli aunty did not speak to me for a whole day because she was very upset because of losing her love messages. I put the diary back in the almirah and joined my family in the dining room.

My mouth started watering at the sight of the lavish spread of food along with my favourite sweets, *jalebis* and *buniya/boondi*. My grandparents were very well aware of the sweet tooth I had since my childhood. There was so much warmth and love around and I savoured every bit of it, but still I felt a kind of emptiness within me.

We all sat shooting the breeze and waiting for the tea after the breakfast. Grandma asked me, 'Cheeru, have you found a girl for you in US, or shall we find out one here?'

I blushed and said, 'Nani ma, let's get over Revati's marriage first.' I left knowing well that now everyone would start pulling my leg. With racing steps, I rushed towards the garden till I stopped, hearing the giggle of ladies.

I sauntered along all alone looking around at the vegetation in full bloom; a bunch of partially ripe *Lichis* hanging from *Lichi* trees, mango trees and so many trees in full bloom. Lost in my thoughts, I kept walking and I was standing in front of a house which looked quite familiar to me. Though the area under the brick cover had increased, and in place of the kitchen garden only a lemon shrub and small chilly plants remained, it did not take me time to recognize the house. It was *Munimji*'s house. *Munimjee* used to assist Grandpa in court. Grandpa was a very renowned lawyer of his time with a roaring practice, and even now clients lined up before him for legal consultation. But he took only selected cases. *Munimji*'s granddaughter, Poornima, who was affectionately called Pinky, was almost my age. Probably, a year younger than me. She was my best friend, and I had never had a friend like her ever since. She used to be my accomplice in the mischief I masterminded. Many times she got her mom's whacks because of me.

I was in front of *Munimji's* grilled iron gate which led to the veranda lined with red bricks in zigzag pattern on one side and a small kitchen garden on the other. Before I could press the doorbell, a beautiful young lady came out from the backdoor in the kitchen garden near the lemon shrub, probably to pluck some lemons. She was wearing peach colour chiffon saree. A dash of pink lipstick and a line of kohl in her eyes made her look gorgeous. She was pushing back the tuft of hair falling on her forehead behind her ear, and her pretty face was revealed like the look of the moon behind the clouds. She appeared to be in a rush. My eyes rested on her face.

*Who is she?* I thought. I remember Mom telling me on phone that Pinky was getting married. So, for sure she was not Pinky. I was conjecturing her to be some relative of Pinky. My eyes forgot to blink looking at her. She was damn beautiful. Looking at her the feeling of emptiness that I experienced also vanished, as if my thirst was quenched with the drop of nectar.

Before I could decide as to whether to go inside or leave, the girl looked around and moved towards the gate. The moment she looked at my face she almost screamed with the excitement, 'Chiranjeev! When did you come?'

I was amazed. *How does she know me, but I have no clues about her?*

Without allowing me any time to get into conversation with her, she opened the gate and led me towards the steps reaching into the grilled semi open lounge. An old man was lying on a Diwan sofa kept towards one side of the room and two sofa chairs were placed perpendicularly.

It didn't take me time to recognize *Munimji*. I went near him and touched his feet for his blessings. The lounge led to the house within through the curtained door. She got me seated near *Munimji* and went inside the house through the curtained door. *Munimji* pulled me near him and kissed my forehead saying, '*Cheeru*, you look even better than your photos.' Every year Mom used to send our photos to Grandpa which he would show to all the people who went to see him, and so we could never become a strange face at Muzaffarpur.

I was getting impatient to know about Pinky, so without giving *Munimji* a chance to engage in further conversation I asked, '*Munimji*, where is Pinky these days?'

*Munimji* gave me a strange look. 'Haven't you met Pinky? She was the one to bring you in, my dear,' he said.

'Oh! So, Poornima has come to see you from her in-law's place', I said with a forced grin on my face. I thought, how nice it would have been if Pinky had not got married. It was not just because of her looks which were as pretty as a picture, but deep down I was feeling an inexplicable sense of satisfaction after seeing her. Probably, this was the feeling I was looking for, and it was the absence of this feeling that caused the feeling of emptiness within me.

Poornima came in holding a tray with some beautiful *moradabadi* brass glasses that had freshly prepared *nimbu pani* with the lemon she plucked from the kitchen garden.

*Munimji* said, 'Pinky, you have not brought *nimbu-pani* for yourself? And where are your parents? Haven't you told them that Chiranjeev is here?'

'*Amma* and *Babuji* have gone with *Bittu* to meet his teacher regarding his board exams. I am waiting for them to arrive then I will go to the school, because Amma told me to be with you while she is away,' Pinky said.

While she was speaking her parents entered from the main gate, and Pinky looked happy and said, '*Daddu*, I am leaving now. And, *Cheeru*, I will come to your house in the evening and meet everyone.' She dashed off waving her hand to bid goodbye.

I mustered all the courage and asked *Munimji*, 'Are Pinky's in-laws in the same town?'

*Munimji* looked surprised and said, 'Which *in-laws*? Pinky never got married.'

'What?' I said with my mouth agape. By that time Pinky's parents had joined us. 'But Mom told me about her wedding, and also that she had received the wedding invitation card too,' I said with further curiosity.

Pinky's mother whom I addressed as *Chachi* started narrating the story. 'Poornima's future in-laws had a long list of demands which we tried to arrange for despite it being beyond our means. Just two days before the marriage a message came from the groom's side that the new couple should be given a send off in the latest model Zen car. [Zen car was the latest model launched by the company which was high in demand and highly priced.] We thought of selling this house to arrange for the car, but Poornima took a tough stand and refused to get married into a greedy family. Like an obedient and a dutiful daughter, she had been saying yes to whatever we said, but after this demand she was adamant not to get married at all. With the money we had arranged for her dowry, she has opened a primary school.'

After hearing the story, I was feeling relaxed and happy, and left the place feeling cheerful.

Poornima came to our house with her parents. We moved outside and started chatting. She asked me, 'Did you see the mango tree we planted together, and how big it has grown?'

Saying this she held my hand and pulled me towards the orchard with the same excitement she did when we were kids.

Her frankness emboldened me. I pulled her hand and looked into her eyes asking, 'Will you marry me?'

She blushed and her eyes looked down for a moment, but she again held my hand and pulled me towards the orchard and brought me in front of the mango tree.

'Wow! It looks majestic!' I said.

The tree had grown quite big and it was full of unripe mangoes.

Pinky said, 'You know I have been nurturing the plant since you left. This tree is a symbol of our friendship. I cannot sleep well, if I don't pay a visit here and spend some time with the tree.'

I went closer to the tree to touch it and feel it more intently. I touched its wide trunk and stroked it.

As I went very close, I spotted some engraving at the back of the wide trunk of the tree which was covered with a bit of dust. I wiped the dust clean to read what was etched on it.

It read:
"Cheeru
TRULY YOURS forever
Pinky"

This must have been etched years back. Though the letters looked dull. Poornima. She hid her face behind both her palms. I removed her palms and said, 'Say this yourself to me.'

She said, *'Yes!* Pinky is truly yours, forever!'

Kaleidoscope